STARS OF BLACK

CONTEMPLATIONS UPON THE PALE KING

BY JULIAN M. MILES

Printed by Createspace, an Amazon.com Company

Available from Amazon.com and other retail outlets

The Lizards of the Host Publishing paperback: www.amazon.co.uk/Stars-Black-Contemplations-Upon-Pale/dp/0957620098/ contains all material from this edition in an A5 format with a revised layout, variant cover art and artwork inside front and rear covers.

The ebook is available for Kindle from Amazon stores worldwide, and for all other devices from Smashwords:

www.smashwords.com/books/view/494651

Design and layout by Julian M. Miles.

Front cover and interior art by Joe Broers. All rights reserved.

Visit us online

Julian M. Miles (a.k.a. Jae): www.lizardsofthehost.co.uk

Joe Broers: zombiequadrille.devianart.com

Lizards of the Host Publishing: www.lothp.co.uk

With respect to

Robert William Chambers

1865 - 1933

There has been no book before or since my reading of 'The King in Yellow' that has estranged me so thoroughly yet so gently. For me, the horror lies in the realisation of the wistful nature of that very detachment.

Of all the iconic characters in weird horror, the King in Yellow seems to inspire the broadest range of emotions and interpretations. This book encapsulates what he brought to me. I can only hope that the works herein strike a resonance with you.

JMM

CONTENTS

SEE THE LIGHTS SHINING

The orchards are teeming and the grasses uncut. Fruit lies where it fell for want of pickers. The buzz of flies is constant and birdsong absent. Over the trees, mountains stand blue-grey; their reliefs sketched in sweeps of snow. Above them, skies so blue they seem impossible outside of computer rendering are marred only by eagles' wings.

Closer to us, the drab tan-and-khaki of the convoy shows where the chalk-scattered road winds between the foundations of the foothills. Some goats forage to one side, oblivious to the bloody ruins of what used to be two men. The herder had raised his staff to point us out to his companion, and one of 'B' company, tired and half-blinded by dust, had cut them both down with a long burst from a vehicle-mounted machine gun. Perceiving everything as a threat is a problem suffered by all who serve long enough out here, where two mountain ranges and four countries meet.

Tajikistan is a beautiful place, but its inhabitants are used to long wars defined in skirmishes by day and offering your enemy shelter against the night. They are an honourable and sturdy folk, used to being invaded often and policed rarely. The country defends its own with breathtaking isolation and savage extremes of weather.

The officer in charge of the convoy was negotiating with the local chief, agreeing honour payments for the two victims. He had been doing that for over two hours, and the long-serving folk amongst the convoy personnel had already resigned themselves to spending the night camped at the roadside. Which meant nervy, tiring sentry duty while the rest of us slept fitfully, feeling exposed and waking at the slightest noise.

Sure enough, as the light faded, we got the order to bivouac as best we could. Watches were doubled up. One of the private military contractors took out a goat, and the smell of roast meat as twilight fell made me drool into my ration pack.

It was barely midnight when the first attack came: shouts from the sentries simultaneous with the percussive rattle of Kalashnikovs. We were still casting about for attackers from other directions when the roar of a vehicle-mounted heavy machine gun settled the matter. A 'small group of pissant amateurs' was the general opinion, grumbled by all trying to settle back to sleep.

An hour later the professionals arrived. We lost four trucks, two patrol vehicles and the armoured command carrier to rocket-propelled grenades during their opening salvo. A multi-pronged attack followed, and everything became what is described as 'fluid' in the reports. Utter chaos is what it meant. A night darker than any would believe, lit only by muzzle flashes, explosions and the occasional small missile trail. The stroboscopic lights burned images into my retinas like black-and-white photographs: a thorn bush, a falling comrade, a robed body flying backwards.

Some time later I found myself lying flat on my back, with my kit blown off, at the edge of a stream. The blurred heavens above me whirled as I gasped for air, winded by the blast that had finished off my team and thrown me over the edge of the bank. I heard rapid conversation in a non-local dialect nearby. It faded as those sent to kill any survivors neglected to check down by the watercourse, where I lay unarmed in a cold sweat.

After lying still for a while, I rolled over and attempted to get my bearings. We had headed north from the convoy, aiming for a slash of shadow that marked a passage through the hills. The distance had been deceptive, and, as we were about to turn back, an outbreak of heavy fire around the convoy - surprisingly far behind - was followed by the attack on us.

I stood up to behold nothing but darkness. Not even a fire burning down by the convoy to help orient myself. So I freed my last knife from its boot-top clip, then took the obvious direction - downhill - and started following the stream-bed. The water itself was teeth-achingly cold, but it dealt with the grit in my mouth and my parched throat.

After heading downstream for a while, I stopped and looked up, trying to identify the source of the unease I felt. The stars above were in negative, like holes in an immense grey cliff, partially veiled by the swirls in a layer of high cloud that had slipped across the sky. I must have cracked my head on a rock when I landed, which would explain my skewed vision. All the more reason to get back sooner rather than later. Looking about, the banks seemed to be lowering, but I still could not see any lights. With a shrug, I stretched to ease the lancing pains in my back, and set off once again.

I entered the end of some ruined orchards, where a fire some months before had scorched the trees to nothing. Figuring myself to be northwest of the road - as the burnt patch of trees had not been visible when we drove in from the southwest - I angled to my left and struck out through the skeletal forest.

Arriving by a lake was the last thing I expected. Seeing a figure walking the shore, I switched grip on my knife and moved cautiously to intercept. I eased off only a little when I saw that the figure wore a dress, but stalled out when I saw it was cut in a formal, almost western, style.

She stopped and I saw that the pale materials and lacy trim complemented her almost-albino complexion. Eyes of limpid blue regarded me with only the faintest trace of surprise. Which was more than I managed. Her eyes lit a fire behind mine, and I nearly dropped my weapon as blood roared in my ears. A flash of old recognition, like a childhood memory surfacing, momentarily staggered me.

Her lips curled into a smile. I was about to look across the lake, for the source of the dim light, when she spoke: "Seek no farther. Turn back and walk away. Cast neither glance nor gaze behind as you do so."

I stammered as I sheathed my blade: "What?"

She walked up to me, dress rustling, and I saw that it was old, with a ragged hem and scorched lace.

"You are somewhere that you cannot be, yet. Turn about and be gone."

I craned my neck to see beyond her, but she slapped my shoulder with surprising force, which spun me about to face the way I came. She stepped up behind me and I tensed, then she laid warm hands upon my lower back and rested cool, soft lips upon my neck.

"Soldier mine, go now. We will meet again, never fear."

Her words were electric and I knew that they were true. A total conviction now lay within the fire her eyes had started.

"Wh-"

"Hush. I am Cariela. No questions. He approaches and you must go."

The push she gave me possessed the barest force, yet I went as if ordered. My body moved with unconscious, trained efficiency as my mind whirled. Before long I became aware of a commotion ahead, as the light became brighter about me. I heard flies buzzing and the light grew to a blinding intensity.

"CLEAR!"

I heard that shout, then lightning struck through my chest. The world blasted from light to dark and back to a familiar, starry sky. A medic I didn't recognise looked down at me with blue eyes that weren't hers.

"Welcome back, soldier. We'll get you patched up, and then it's just waiting for evac."

I grinned and then realised that I couldn't feel my legs. As my eyes went wide I saw hers flick to one side. An injector stung my neck and everything faded away.

Two months later, I sit on a neatly trimmed lawn in my wheelchair, looking across a lake. My legs are here, but I left my ability to walk in Tajikistan. They say that the piece of shrapnel that severed my lower spine should have killed me when it came out. Something had ameliorated and cauterised the wound. Something that left a small, perfect, handprint as a burn-scar. Some pointedly anonymous people had spent a long time asking me portentously vague questions about that, to no avail.

That lake is not on any map, current or ancient. They told me I must have been 'off the reservation' in more ways than one, but presented me with no explanations. My body had been found the evening after the attack, right outside the base that the convoy had left a week before. But for that mystifying, merciful transit, I would have died.

After they told me that, I knew that all I had to do was wait. Cariela will find me when it's time to walk with her under stars like caves in the sky. Which will be when it's time for us to go to the place with lights that shine across that lake.

COLD LAVENDER

The Garrick Playhouse was as good as it got for the lower classes in the East End of London. Histrions past their prime played alongside aspiring stars and no-hopers, all aiming to make a penny or two. We performed classic plays, simplified for the rabble, or local works that told straightforward morality tales. Whatever we put on had to be easily understood by the audience, who were usually near-bereft of their senses on the cheap potables they had guzzled on the way to the show.

This month it was 'The Robes of Yellow Death', a mutilation of Poe's eponymous work. It was set in a whorehouse, which was fitting as the scantily clad cast were either dollymops taking a night off or bangtails looking to catch the eye of their next thrill. Only two lads shared the stage with 'em. The big fellow was Mackey; a monstrous stevedore who no-one would have guessed was a mandrake, due to his enviable manliness. He used it to good effect playing Hector, the owner of the bordello - the part that took the place of Prospero. When he finally toppled to the stage, after being struck dead of fright by the Yellow Plague – played by Clarence, the

7

other lad - the whole playhouse fair shook, and dust sifted from the rafters.

Dicky, the doorman, sniffed as Mackey finished another pre-death diatribe: "I swear he takes longer to die than a toff with consumption. I thought the death was meant to be 'swift, like a man gun-shot'?"

It was. 'Hector' should have said his line and keeled over, with none of the ad-libbed, wheezing lamentations before he went. But the audience loved his saucy takes on current events amongst London's rich and shameless, rendered in gasping detail with his 'dying' breaths.

My cousin Charlie was the playwright for most of the penny-ha'penny shows around town, and a couple of his had even graced the stage at the Colosseum Saloon, for all that they were only early-afternoon punter bait. He understood that clipping Mackey's ad-libs would lessen the pull for the crowd.

Eventually, another tawdry spectacle came to an end. We roused the sleepers and tossed the drunks, then set to cleaning what needed to be clean and tarting up whatever needed to look clean. It was into this relative peace that the heated argument between Charlie and Clarence echoed.

"You can't quit. We're on a roll!" Charlie was livid, that much I could tell.

"Bugger yer prancing about, I've got a proper job." Clarence was not swayed.

"Who else would let you act, you tosspot?"

He had a fair argument with that one.

"Don't care no more. Stagehand at the Royal Coburg is what I'm for."

The New Vic had been looking? Wish I'd known that.

"The Blood Tub is welcome to you."

Low blow, cousin.

"Then give me my teviss and I'll be away, you skinny runt."

Fat chance. Only the women would be getting a shilling as pay for the run. They acted better than Clarence, and their only practice had been on their backs.

"What chink? There's no divvy until we finish the run and that's a fortnight off."

I put down my broom and moved quietly round the corner, into the shadows behind Clarence.

"Then you'll pay me from yer own pocket or I'll-"

He got no further. I had seen his elbow bend sharply in the wan candlelight. Trapping his wrist, as he grabbed the hefty dagger tucked into the back of his britches, I dragged him out into the main hall.

"You like yer shivs too much, Clarence. Bugger off. Come back at the end of the run and you'll get your divvy, unless you try any funny stuff between now and then."

As Clarence reached the doors to the foyer, I hurled his shiv to stick in the lintel above his head. He ducked as it hit, then looked back at me in a mix of surprise and fear.

"Charlie is the good lad in this family. You'll answer to me if you play up."

Clarence nodded, see-sawed his shiv out of the woodwork, and left. I turned to Charlie, who looked like someone had kicked him low and hard.

"Come on Charlie, he's not the only useless histrion around these parts."

Charlie's face brightened: "You're right. Tomorrow morning, bright and early, we'll get ourselves a new player."

There went my night on the randy with one of the 'actresses'.

As if obeying his command, next morning was blindingly bright. But the combination of unexpected warmth and low tide made the stench worse than usual. Charlie dragged me down narrow ways, boots squelching in tepid muck, knocking on this door and that. Heaven alone knows how he knew where to go, but go we did - until my legs ached. Eventually, we bagged a gamecock named Tamanny Beck, recently in from somewhere godawful and even possessed of a smattering of French to impress our punters with. He was a tall lad with shoulders of differing height, but moved easy enough. Charlie gave him a shilling and Beck, as he liked to be called, was ours to command for this play and the next.

He was also a quick study. Charlie had him up to speed, and I have to admit, he showed just what a lump Clarence had been. I never really got the idea of 'stage presence' until I saw him. He wandered onto the stage, into the throng of women, and his height marked him out, while the oddly stiff gait he adopted made a stranger of him. Charlie was delighted.

"Beck! That's enough. We're done. Dressing at six tonight."

We cleared out the bangtails - the dollymops didn't get here until dressing time, they were working – and had just sat down to a spot of lunch when Beck came back, a delightful filly holding his hand.

"Mister Peterson, my Sienna has always wanted to take the stage, and I said you would be good enough to give her a go."

Charlie went rigid with affront. Bloody hell, asking that was a bit forward for someone we hadn't known from cock-crow to last light yet.

"Beck, she's very pretty, but I really can't -"

"I know, Mister Peterson. But I've got something you might be interested in. For giving Sienna a chance, like. It's a play."

He held up a roll of parchment, and Charlie almost pounced on him. I heard the paper crack as he unrolled it. Charlie read a bit, then looked up at me with a ridiculous smile on his face.

"It says *Rex in Crocus*, Brent. It's older than the copy of *Le Roi en Jaune* that Davidson had."

I recognised the name 'Davidson'. He'd been the histrion who took Charlie under his wing, until the old coot finally drank himself under the lavender.

"That's nice, Charlie. How about you tell me about it in the Queen's English?"

Charlie laughed and slapped Beck on the back: "Sienna can watch tonight and join the troupe tomorrow. Good enough?"

Beck nodded as Sienna beamed.

I snapped my fingers: "Charlie! Rex what?"

He blinked: "It's a classic, got a bad outing a few times and picked up a repute far worse than the Scottish play. I never thought to see its like here."

"Will it make us chink?" That's the problem with histrions and those who write for them: precious little grasp of the essentials.

Charlie paused: "I'll have to make it easier for the crowd, but they're rowdy all the way through Robes of Yellow Death. I adapted the character of Yellow Plague from what I remembered of the lead in *Le Roi en Jaune*."

A piece of luck, then. Or not: "The play Beck gave you has a different title, Charlie."

"Yes, it does. That's because it's an earlier manuscript, written in Latin. *Le Roi en Jaune* is French."

"And you can read Latin?"

Charlie shrugged: "I have enough Medieval Latin to get the guts out of this. If this manuscript had been in Classical Latin – Davidson said it was called *Regem in Flavum* - I wouldn't know where to start. But I can use this to fill the gaps in what I remember of his telling of the French one. We could have something to bring in goodly amounts of chink. Might even attract some toffs, and you know how they spend. Remember, our stage will still have a few dollymops and bangtails. Introductions cost, last time I heard. And our ladies won't need a dinner and an outing before they get grassy."

Beck's cheeks coloured and he rushed Sienna out, muttering darkly about our lack of manners.

I liked the sound of Charlie's lay. A chance at proper chink would make a nice change. Plus, I could set a few nobblers to mug the toffs on their way home, and take a cut of the hauls for doing so.

Beck's opening night was a success, and we found no sleepers after the show, which was a first. The next afternoon Sienna came in and - to our surprise, and Beck's horror - handed back better than she got from the girls. That filly had a gutter mouth on her, when she was minded to use it.

By dressing-time that night, she was well in, and when she came on stage the catcalls nearly lifted the roof. A toffer at the Garrick? That was a first. Many men who whistled got a beating from their women, egged on with encouragement and advice from those about. For a while, the audience was a better show than the one on stage.

Over the next two weeks, we made more chink than ever, but I kept seeing hard lads, the sort that toffs hired to do their dirty work, hanging about. I started to carry both of my shivs, but didn't say a thing to Charlie. He was spending a lot of time burning the midnight oil, running on gin, writing up this new play. Said his adaptation was going to be called The Black Lake, so it didn't attract the wrong kind of attention. Whatever that was, he wouldn't say.

The last night of The Robes of Yellow Plague damn near brought the house down. We were all happy as we cleared up, until I heard Beck shout and Sienna scream. I raced to the stage door and there was Sienna, being manhandled toward a black carriage by a pair of the hard lads I had noticed.

The first was down, gurgling his last around one of my shivs, as I set about the other. We had a right jolly before I set him under the lavender good and proper. Beck was shouting something as I tore the door of the carriage open, the cabby's whip wound about my fist where I had pulled it from his hand.

Inside the carriage was a portly chap who gabbled something fast in French. I was about to put shiv to toff when Charlie shouted: "Hold hard!"

This being the first time Charlie had called me out of a jolly before everyone was laid out, I stayed my hand. The toff regained a little colour, and I waited with interest, shiv at the ready, for things to run clear.

Charlie surprised me by gabbling right back at the toff in French, and I heard Sienna's name mentioned several times. They had a right natter before Charlie ran back inside and came out holding the parchment Beck had given him. Next thing I know, the toff has the parchment and Charlie has the toff's purse. The whole damn thing. The toff just gave him the lot.

As the carriage clattered off - me having given the driver back his whip - Charlie did a little jig, before waving us all back inside.

"Take a look, Brent." He held out the open bag to me. Inside were gold coins. I looked 'em over carefully: they were all proper sovereigns - a dozen of 'em. We were in the chink!

I looked up at Charlie: "How the bloody hell did you pull that off? And give me one; I've got hard lads to disappear."

Charlie grinned and shook his head, giving me a couple of shillings after closing the bag. He looked at Beck: "That was Sienna's former owner. She did a runner a while back, and Beck hid her out. Right now, she's free and we're rich. We can afford to spruce this place up for the The Black Lake."

I raised a hand: "Easy now. That's a goodly sum, but it's going to have to go a long way if your play doesn't cut the mustard."

Charlie grinned: "I told Mister Defrou about what I was doing with the manuscript. He said he knew of several gentlemen who could be interested enough to attend the opening night, and that they would pay top mark for the crow's nest if they did."

The crow's nest being the upper balcony, from which myself and Dicky usually watched the shows.

"I guess me and Dicky can mix with the punters for a night. But first, I have to sink a pair of toughs. See you in the morning."

The Thames gained a couple of floaters, and I got more from their pockets than I paid the lads helping me. A good night, all in all.

Charlie spent the next month working on the play. He confided in me that he could work better with the manuscript gone. It had been disturbing in places, he said. Quite how that worked, I had no idea. But if Charlie was happier, all well and good.

I didn't spot it when Sienna took up with him, but Beck gave it away a couple of days later: stalking about with a face like a dray horse on a wet day. When he told me, I think I hurt his feelings when I burst out laughing: "Come on, Beck. If you were ever going to do diddly with Sienna, it would have been before you brought her here. Saving her from Defrou, getting her all the way to London town, and you still hadn't got her grassy? You were never going to, and you know it. Her settling on Charlie is the best thing. You can join me in tupping the 'actresses'."

He laughed at that. Most things you'd consider bad have a silver lining. But you usually need someone to point it out to you. So we worked to turn Charlie's godawful drawings into scenery, and that was where we met a slight problem.

One afternoon, I found Charlie measuring up the stage and looking worried.

"What's up, Charlie?"

"We're going to have to plank over the front row." He was serious.

"The hell as like we are. What do you need the space for?"

"The Black Lake. It has to be front right so the witch can use the trapdoor."

"Stop. Losing two dozen punters because you need the false lake to be bigger? And a witch? Have you gone to the Scottish play completely? We have enough problems when the preacher comes, to make sure we're not corrupting his flock, anyway. It cost a pretty penny to keep him off while The Robes of Yellow Plague was on. And why do we need a witch, anyway?"

Charlie looked dreamily off to my left, like he was watching his play on a stage the width of the gallery: "She emerges from the lake with white hair to show that she has shed her sins. But they were so great that it turned the lake black, forever. We open with that, and close with Sienna's character going down into the lake to save her love."

I may be a hard lad with not a drop of histrion in me, but I saw something plain at that moment.

16

"So the lake is only at the beginning and end? Where does the rest of the play happen?"

Charlie waved behind him, toward stage left: "On the veranda of the manor that overlooks the lake."

The hell it would: "Charlie, why not have the whole play in the living room, so the audience is where the lake would be? Then we can have the walkway on stage right as the veranda, or even a jetty."

Charlie blinked: "What about the witch?"

Sienna had quietly come up behind Charlie. She put an arm round his waist and said: "Have one of the guests telling the legend to the gathering as the opening piece, with everybody lit from the back of the stage. Then you can drop back to that motif and people will know that it is something from the time before."

She was very good. I even understood most of what she said. Charlie got it all, and laughed in delight, before kissing Sienna - then fumbled in embarrassment as he remembered that I was till there.

"Uh, Brent..."

I grinned: "I know, cousin. You make a pretty couple."

Sienna giggled and Charlie blushed and that was the end of that. No more was said of planking or painted lakes.

Charlie changed the name of the play to 'The Black Manor'. The sign-writers liked that: they could work with a fancy house. Lakes were a bit flat and dull.

The rehearsals were odd, to start with. Everyone had a sense of being involved in something special. After a week, they had it down and the work turned to fun again. Charlie sent a runner to Mister Defrou, and I spent two days tarting up the crows nest.

It was the night before opening night when Beck came to find me.

"Bloke from Defrou for you. Actually, he's for Sienna, but I thought you'd want to handle it."

"You're damn right I do." I headed for the stage door. Fortunately, I knew this hard lad. We had done some time together at Her Majesty's pleasure.

"Brent. I thought it might be you when me toff said that I was more likely to get you coming out than the filly."

I grinned: "Smart man, your toff. So, what's this about?"

"He said that he kept something of Sienna's when she ran away. He feels bad about it and wants her to have it back. Says it belonged to her mother."

I knew that Sienna's mum had died while in service, after being with the family for a good while. Nice of the old gent to let things go at last.

"I'll make sure she gets it, and you tell his nibs that she said thank you."

His turn to grin: "Wasn't going to say owt else."

He went his way, and I went to find Charlie. I might know how hard lads think, but women are a mystery to me. I expected that Charlie would know, and he did.

"You give it to her tomorrow night, before she goes on stage. It'll mean more if you tell her then."

I didn't understand that either. Charlie was her toff: I could see it in the way she looked at him. But if he said I should do it, and I should do it the following night, then I would.

The next evening, I knocked on the ladies' changing-room door and asked for Sienna. She came out in a loose robe, her makeup half-done and a questioning look on her face.

"What is it, Brent?"

I offered up the little box that had been sent: "Mister Defrou sent this. He said that it was a keepsake of your mother's. He felt it only fair that you have it back for tonight."

Sienna looked up at me, tears forming in her eyes: "My mother's? I had nothing of her. Now I do."

She opened the box to reveal a gold ring. I looked it over as she stood gasping: a thick band of gold made up of twisted strands, topped with a cabochon-cut black stone in an eight-claw setting. Cut into the face of the stone was a curious symbol, vaguely square in outline, inlaid with pure gold. It was a fetching piece and worth a fortune, but the symbol that topped it struck me as decidedly queer.

Sienna fair squealed in delight and slipped it onto the middle finger of her right hand, before darting back into the changing rooms, whereupon I heard a clamour start up as she showed off her heirloom.

Job done, I retired to the foyer, just in time to escort a second group of toffs up to the crows nest. This group even had a couple of ladies with them. They tipped well, and seemingly for every little thing, plainly put out of sorts by the rough setting for their evening's entertainment.

Back downstairs Dicky closed and locked the outer doors, then we closed the doors between foyer and main hall behind us. It was show time.

The Black Manor was quite something. Charlie had taken Mackey's ad-libs and worked the scurrilous and the witty into the play as conversations between the guests. The audience always had something to laugh about, a bounder to heckle or a fop to ridicule. Cheers went up whenever Beck's character, Robard, intervened to save a guest from the schemes of one of the dastardly types, of which there were several.

A pair of Mister Defrou's sovereigns had gotten us half-a-dozen quite good repertory players. They acted their parts, and exchanged asides with the audience, without breaking sweat. Charlie had let them work out the bout of boxing - needed to settle a gentleman's argument - and their experience showed. People were picking sides and acting like the stage had become a ring.

Sienna was radiant as Clarissa, and when she and Robard acted out their moment of unrequited love, I actually saw a couple of matrons sniffling.

And so the play moved smoothly, with bad people getting just desserts and good people coming out on top. But as tragedies must, the Yellow King was to take Clarissa away, and Robard was to realise that he loved her after all, only to have lost her forever.

Charlie had set the piece well, with Beck set to change into the robes he had worn for the Yellow Plague, then simply add a tall crown that the smithy had knocked up for us.

The first encounter was to be the Yellow King passing unnoticed through the gathering, pausing only to regard Clarissa. The second, and final, encounter was set on the veranda, when the Yellow King offered her a place as his Red Queen. She would accept and depart with him, there being nothing left at the Black Manor after Robard had spurned her.

The gathering moved about on stage like all of us imagined toffs at parties behaved. Then, from stage right, the Yellow King entered. Charlie must have decided to save the crown for the last scene, but having the people move out of his way, so he never had to go around anyone, was a nice touch.

He paused, head turning slowly, to regard Sienna where she stood, just forward of centre stage. With deliberate steps, somehow laden with menace, he moved closer to her. A hush fell over the audience. In a clever ad-lib, with the gentlest of movements, he took her chin lightly between thumb and forefinger.

Sienna played along with it, and reacted as if a steel trap had slammed shut upon her jaw. As she thrashed wildly, a shriek of strangled agony tore from her lips. A few screams from the audience echoed hers. As her hand came up, he caught it in his offhand, palming her fingers and languidly driving the hand down. Then his head shook, as if in disappointment, and, with the release of his touch, she fell like a discarded cloak to lie motionless upon the stage.

He moved off, actors still casually moving from his path rather than he having to avoid them. As he exited stage left, the cast seemed to suddenly become aware that Sienna had not stirred from her repose, and rushed to her side. I saw Bethany - a dollymop who could really act - touch Sienna and pull her fingers back as if burned.

She looked out into the audience: "Oh, Gawd. Is there a doctor in the house?"

Then I saw the Yellow King enter again from stage right, this time wearing a tall crown, only to falter and stop at the sight of Sienna's prone form. Dread pushed me from my post by the doors, and I rushed to the stage, leaping up to skid to a stop at Sienna's side.

I heard Charlie's cry: "Is she alright?"

Sienna was about as far from alright as you could get, in my experience. She was stone dead and already cold.

I pointed toward stage left: "Get the coppers! Stop the murderer in the yellow robes!"

From that point, things dissolved into chaos.

It was just after dawn the following day when the last policeman let himself out into the yellow-grey murk of a London Particular. We sat about the stage, Dicky and I, Charlie and Beck. A bottle of gin had come and gone, and Charlie had cried himself out. Distantly, I could hear Bethany sobbing, down in the ladies' changing-room.

No-one knew what had killed Sienna, but I had spotted pretty quick that the ring was missing. A quick search turned up the box, but the fancy piece was gone with the killer, and the killer had gone from stage left to clean getaway with an ease that raised my hackles.

Monsieur Defrou had disappeared that night as well, but before rumour and suspicion could ruin his family, his body was fished out of the Thames. Dead before he went in, and not a mark on him. The toffs who attended the play closed ranks, and I got nothing but a solid beating when I went asking direct questions.

Charlie never wrote again. Eventually, he went back to Bristol. I went back to vamping, taking Dicky with me. Beck came along for a while but his heart wasn't in it. After he stopped a bullet in the leg one night, he quit London as soon as he could walk without bleeding.

When I got the news that Charlie had tucked himself under the lavender by jumping off Clifton Suspension Bridge, it was the last straw. I took ship for America within a month. No-one could point out to me the silver lining hidden behind the events at the end of The Black Manor, because there wasn't one. America seemed like a place where a man could lose himself, and try to lose some memories in so doing.

EXPRESS

I hate them all. The men with their expensive suits and loud voices, the women with their incessant gossip and girly squeals. The latest fashions, the next car, new knick-knacks, then the problems at work and the incredulous tones used as the *obvious* solutions are stated for all to agree with.

They're hot and sweaty and their deodorant gave up on the tube to London Bridge. They smell of after-work drinks 'with the team', and the reek of their fast food makes me want to vomit. The containers perch on top of the latest business periodicals – always the ones that the general public can't get.

Then they settle and laptops open, tablets slide out and coffee cups are moved like chess pieces, as the tables fill with the paraphernalia that clutters mundane lives. The chatter becomes sporadic, but then I can hear the infants complaining to parents too stupid to avoid a commuter train for the return from their puerile day trip.

I used to be like them, but I have escaped. I found my calling in the hand of a tramp sleeping in the shadows of Southwark Cathedral.

Like all of my 'colleagues', I didn't pay any attention to the dossers that littered the ways to and from work. But this one wore the shabby remains of a quality suit. I had stopped, Blackberry ready for an emergency call, to see if he'd mugged someone I knew. Then, to my horror, I recognised him. It was Michael Stanley, a fallen star who had been escorted from the premises a week ago last Tuesday. Rumours had flown fast and inaccurate: I'd only reported him for littering the copying room on every evening of the previous week. There was no way in United Kingdom employee law that photocopying stuff after hours could get someone the gross-misconduct march.

A twinge of leftover guilt had made me crouch down and prod his shoulder. He started awake with a shrill cry that made my blood run cold. As he straightened and blinked at me, I saw that he had been draped across a battered briefcase.

"Toby?" He was squinting like an old man.

I smiled: "Hello Mike. Want to get a decent meal?" It was the least I could do – and the quickest way to get away from him.

He shook his head: "Can't. No time. All time. Nothing left." He fumbled with the catches on the briefcase. Plunging his hand inside, he came out with a crumpled pamphlet: "Read this. Explanation. Get what you need."

At that, he pushed himself up, with surprising vigour, and all but ran into the dusk. I checked the time and sprinted for the train, pamphlet in one hand, season ticket in the other.

Collapsed on the train, I felt a wash of disproportionate relief. To be stuck in the city for one minute longer than necessary – especially on a deserted platform – was torture. It usually ended in being sentenced to travel to Brighton; standing in cattle-class with crazies and drunks from Bedford.

I lifted my hand and looked at the bundle of paper wadded up in it. By chance, I had settled at a table claimed by three hardcore real-book readers. Silence spread from them in ruffled waves toward the garrulous, or those with loud headphones. Tonight seemed to be one of those rare occasions when it actually worked.

Flattening the creased pages on the table, I unravelled the crumpled mass to reveal an A6-sized chapbook, sporting a twin-stapled spine and neatly trimmed corners. The texture of the paper was familiar to my touch. So this was what he'd been making in the copying room.

The cover was blank, but on the inside of it was printed what I took to be the title:

THE BOOK OF
NIGHT'S DREAMING

Checking inside the equally blank back cover, I found a strange passage, similar to what would appear upon a book jacket:

Should the river slow
or divagation beset,
be reassured.
Whether churls decry
or gods forfend,
pay no heed.

These pages provide
all that you need.
Take this as your guide:
let the book decide.

Mike had pinned the covers inside out, for some reason. Without pausing, I turned to the first page and read until the words danced before my eyes, so accurate and cutting were the observations within.

Before we reached East Croydon, I had completed the book twice. The second time I read it, details I had missed sprang out. I left the train at Worthing with tentative steps, stunned into doddering silence. The book was only twenty pages cover-to-cover, but the insights I had gained from reading it six times were incredible.

By this morning, I had read the book many more times, eschewing sleep in favour of enlightenment. Pausing only to shower, I headed for the train to London Bridge. It was on there that I noticed the brittleness of routine in those about me. Their pathetic obeisance to the gods of 'more'. I listened to them spew their platitudes and plot their petty office triumphs and felt sick to the pit of my stomach, so I took refuge in the book.

The day in the office was purgatory, alleviated only by trips to the Gents so I could gain a moment's respite to read in a stall. Even then, I had to cram my ears with toilet roll to shut out the banal bravado and powerless spite occurring outside.

Memories merge with the present, and the homeward journey has become intolerable. I rise from my seat and head towards the toilet: a

herculean trek through five carriages because the first WC is out of
service. By the time I make it, and politely wait my turn - every
nerve screaming for me to beat and tear at those ahead of me - we are
pulling out of Hassocks.

Taking the seat, I face the curved wall-cum-door and stuff my ears
with toilet tissue. Settling to give myself a half-hour of respite from
the lowing mob outside, I take a deep breath and open the booklet.
As I flick through the pages, two words catch my eye: 'Clayton
Tunnel'.

Strange. I don't recall reading that before, and we're just
approaching it; the longest tunnel on the line, situated between
Hassocks and Preston Park. I open the booklet flat to concentrate
better on the page:

> He had risen from mean streets to work in
> the heart of the metropolis, financing his
> transition with the valuables looted from the
> bodies in a tsunami-torn Sri Lankan village.

> But even he realised that being fain to
> attract the pale king's attention, as the
> stygian darkness of Clayton Tunnel hurtled
> toward him, was utter folly.

How the-! What is this?
What happened to the lights?

Stoic commuters, locked into the pastimes that while away their
journey home, are unable to blithely ignore the incoherent shouting
coming from the WC. When the shouting crescendos in a shrill
scream, heads turn and glances are exchanged. As the train exits the

tunnel, and the last rays of the sun illumine the carriage, the door to the WC remains closed. Those nearby are discomfited by the memory of what they heard, but none will meet another's glance.

Finally, as Preston Park nears, a man sighs, rests his magazine on the luggage rack, and knocks on the door: "You alright, mate? We heard you shouting. Are you okay?"

When no reassurance is forthcoming, he looks at his companion, the first stirrings of concern showing upon his face: "Better call the conductor, Andy. It's gone awful quiet in there."

The tramp stood on tip-toe and screamed so deep and so loud that people swore they had heard the roar of a train. Passers-by flinched and several grabbed for their phones, either to film his agony or to call for help. By the time the first phone had been brought to bear, or to ear, Michael Stanley had toppled.

Supine on the lawn, under the great tree in the grounds of Southwark Cathedral, his expression was one of peace. His eyes were jaundiced orbs, and there was blood upon his smiling lips.

Where his briefcase had fallen open, little booklets whirled away on a wind that gusted, without warning, to urgently ruffle bystanders' clothing. Some folk paused to watch the pamphlets rise into the evening sky, until the snapping of white pages became indistinguishable from the wings of pigeons and gulls.

Bleeding Heart and Hourglass

The sun has risen. More correctly, the tinge to the fog swirling about my boat has lightened, to a sickly yellow-grey, from the ghostly grey murk of a short while ago. It must be time to break my fast upon a coal-like lump of hardtack, moistened with a swig of rum.

Days have become a questionable thing in my little world of dull grey waters and dull grey fog, both changing shade in some semblance of dawn and dusk. I have no shortage of victuals, so I'll not be dying of thirst or hunger for a little while longer.

The question of where I am has also become moot. We were far from any charted routes, and, some said, far from any uncharted routes that even a crazed buccaneer would consider. So I feel safe in concluding that I am, sooner or later, doomed.

A legend of hidden treasure is what led me into these dire straits, and I have to confess that I was as eager as any of the crew when Vertho came aboard with his map and his strange liquor. After an afternoon and evening listening to what he had to say, while sampling what he had to offer, I think we would have cheerfully assailed the Gates of Hell if he had intimated that more of his brew could only be obtained from Lucifer himself.

As it was, the 'Jenny May' left Tortuga on the dawn tide two days later, provisioned, armed, and assured that all wenches had been put ashore. We sailed for weeks across a sea that could have been ordered by God for the joy of life under a buccaneer's colours. Clear skies and fair winds wafted us apace toward a destination that existed only as a location on Captain Rigson's charts.

I, as sponsor, knew well enough to leave the sailing to the sailors. When something required purchasing, paying off, or haggling to death, my skills would be required. In all other circumstances, I was a man of leisure living upon a ship full of ugly men with brutal pursuits, both at work and at play.

The ban on wenches aboard did not, of course, extend to include me. I kept the little thing in my quarters, busy with maintaining my wardrobe, when not busy entertaining me. It was a reckless defiance, and I would bemoan my lot, were it not that Sally paid full tariff for my arrogance. Suffice to say that the first mate betrayed me to the Captain. He was a callous man, even amongst the host of merciless men aboard, and locked me in my quarters while the crew had their way with her. When they were done, they tossed her body overboard with the slops. The dirge they chanted while they dealt with her fair raised my hackles. Some vile shanty to avert the ill-fortune destined for ships that sailed with a woman aboard, I presumed.

After that, I was not so welcome. All of my work to be grudgingly accepted had been undone. I had demonstrated that I was not even remotely a son-of-the-sea, just some fancy landsman who thought he could do as he pleased, and damn the ways of seafaring folk.

I took to spending a lot of my time in my quarters, which abutted the Captain's. For all his savagery, Rigson liked books. While his tastes ran to bawdy or brightly illustrated, a chest in his cabin yielded some esoteric discoveries: no doubt the proceeds of pillaging other vessels.

It was during one of my forays to peruse the reading material on offer that I chanced upon Vertho pawing through that chest.

"Good afternoon, Mister Vertho. You seem to be looking for something."

Vertho jumped as if stabbed in the rump. He landed, and drew steel as he spun. Before ought more was said, I found myself backed up into the corner by the door to my cabin, the point of a curved blade resting lightly upon my Adam's apple.

"I may be lookin'. I may not. What business be it of yours?"

I had been about to volunteer that I had several of the books from the chest in my cabin. Given my brusque treatment, I chose reticence: "None, good Vertho. My apologies."

He nodded his head at that and smiled as he stepped away, sheathing his sword. I lingered by the door, until he looked at me and barked: "Still here?"

I returned to my room, closing the door and making a loud display of locking it. I heard chuckling before the sound of rummaging recommenced. While he searched, his curses revealing a specific object to his quest - and no luck in finding it - I decided to look through the books I had borrowed.

They were all essentially poor fare, no doubt works of repute at their time of printing, but singularly lacking in appeal to a modern man of words, such as myself. The only exception was what I had thought to be some kind of classic tragedy, despairing that the book had been rent asunder at some point. Upon closer examination, I found it to be the first act of a play, titled and written in Greek. I was sure that the last word of the title, 'Kítrino', meant 'king'. But, beyond that, my grasp of the language was insufficient to do more than guess that the English title would consist of three or four words, with the last of them being 'King'.

I had barely done puzzling over that, when the door between my cabin and the Captain's was kicked inwards. Vertho stormed in, eyes lighting upon the torn book in my hand.

"That's mine!" One hand reached toward me. The other grasped the hilt of his sword, conveying clear intent. I sighed and extended my arm slowly, the ruined tome held lightly. He wrenched it from my grasp. Without another word, he slammed out of mine and the Captain's cabins.

Rigson took some quieting over the ruined door, but coins soothe where words fail, and we ended the evening amicably, over a glass or two of rum.

"What d'ye make of Vertho?" the question came, apropos of nothing.

I thought carefully before replying: "He is a buccaneer turned something else. I have no doubt that he answers to another."

"An agent? Of whom?"

I shrugged: "I have no idea. Out here, it is of no matter. The seas are clear from horizon to horizon; day in, day out. Whoever he serves awaits his return."

Rigson nodded: "He mutters of a tome that will complete the puzzle which we sail toward answering. Did he get it from you?"

"Only half. The back of it was torn away."

Rigson grimaced: "I remember a scrappy ketch too far from anywhere. The crew fought like demons, while a few escaped in a lateen-rigged longboat. They had the wind and were well away before we took the ketch. I took that book because it had obviously meant something to the lass who clutched it to her breast, even thought it was torn and she lay dying. We only got petty loot from the ketch to boot. Stood off and sank it afterwards, because we'd found an officer's gear on board. Nothing good comes from letting the authorities know you took some of their own. Better it be just another missing ship."

I nodded and let the conversation drift to other topics, while my mind contemplated a fleeing longboat and the fortunate souls within.

It was barely a week later that we fell becalmed, about as far south as we could be, while remaining in the tropics. As the days ground on, the men became fractious. Captain Rigson had to kill one who became demented.

It was into this atmosphere, of languid calm surrounding burning frustration, that Vertho made his proposal. The fragment he had retrieved from me completed the book he carried. There were cheers as he announced that he now knew exactly where we should be headed, and the glad tidings, that journey's end lay no more than a few days away, worked well to alleviate the sullenness of the crew.

When he suggested that all aboard hear the play that the book contained, there was scepticism. After a discussion with the Captain, the two of them announced that rum casks would be broached and a party made of the whole affair.

There is nothing in my experience that matches the sight of the 'Jenny May', becalmed under a full August moon, her decks swarming with deadly buccaneers all pretending airs and graces, while dolphin and kelp cooked over coals on the forecastle. Rum was circulating, but while many were merry, none were drunk. The ridiculous nature of the diversion had brought all over to participate, with little grumbling.

After the food was served, Vertho broached the last two casks of the brew with which he had persuaded us to engage upon this foray, and received a roar of approbation. Both were swiftly consumed, and the euphoric camaraderie it engendered settled upon us all.

Vertho moved to stand upon the aftcastle, book in hand. With a voice that should have graced the stage, he launched into the tale of what he announced as 'The King in Yellow'.

For the first act, a listening peace settled over the deck, and all was silent bar calls for the passing of the rum. I sat behind Vertho with my back against the stern rail, smoking a pipe and sipping rum with moderation. I considered myself to be only slightly tipsy, but even in that state I felt the effect of the words. The playwright had been truly inspired.

As the second act drew on, I felt discomfort. There were many places where key detail was only obliquely given, and in a way that prompted the mind to fill the gaps with discomfiting exactitude. If that was how it affected me, I dread to think what the minds of those below conjured to fill the voids.

The words kept coming, Vertho seemingly immune to the needs of thirst, hunger or rest. His voice rose and fell, taking the parts of man, woman, commoner or king, with consummate ease. It was a triumphant performance: something that should have been feted, while at the same time damned. Would that I had not realised the depths which his recounting plumbed, the dissonances and disgraces lifted from the listener's own mind, the futility traced lightly through man's every endeavour. It was poisonous. It was haunting. It was glorious. And as it approached culmination, I am ashamed to say that I fainted: a combination of rum and kelp upon one who had never experienced seaweed as a foodstuff, I suspect.

When I awoke, I thought it was still night. Then I saw the fog swirling across the deck of the aftcastle and heard the cries of the damned below. Night and day were suddenly immaterial. As I crawled toward the stairs, I became aware of Vertho, sat with his back against the wheelpost. The book was clutched tight in his grasp and he rocked like a child in pain, tears streaming down his face from eyes screwed tight shut. I could smell the urine that soaked his britches.

Looking down onto the deck was like peering into a vision of hell. The gamut of human emotions were being enacted below, by lone performers or groups, with delirious consent or unwilling, it made no never mind. I

saw Taff the cabin boy in one of Sally's gowns, being ill-used in ways
that mocked my supposed worldliness. I saw Captain Rigson flogging a
side of meat that had been a man. I saw and heard Tomlinson singing
like an angel from the barrel he stood upon. I saw fights and weeping
consolations, heard diatribes and lullabies. But one thing slowly dawned
upon me: no matter how virtuous the emotions expressed, all were
working toward a frenzied culmination that promised unthinkable
atrocities.

I flitted like a thief around scenes better suited to Purgatory, avoiding
all, as I provisioned the captain's boat, which was fastened in a pulley
rig at the stern. That being done, I took what I dared from around about
- my one sally below decks having determined me to avoid those cramped,
poorly-lit hells. Lowering the boat blistered my hands and nearly
plunged me into the still waters prow-first, but I managed it. Without a
backward glance, I set to the oars and rowed until exhaustion took me.

And so here I sit, adrift without hope, having fled a hopeless and
damned ship. This notebook is all I have to while away the hours until
sight of land or the advent of death succours me. I shall wrap this
missive in oilcloth ere my time comes.

If you should see a Manila galleon decked out as a man-o'-war, flying
the bleeding heart and hourglass under crossed cutlasses, or see the name
'Jenny May' upon a prow or stern, make course away; for you may be
assured that nothing sane stalks her decks.

May God be ever with you.

Yours faithfully,
Llewellyn Reece-Mortimer.

TATTERS

The leaves are tinged with premature autumn shades by the few rays of the setting sun that penetrate the lowering grey clouds. I turn off the quiet B-road and the sunlight disappears as the rain starts to hammer down. The long, slow cruise up the wide gravel drive lets my mind wander back to the day that Lathan Dove first came to me, five years ago.

He was a nondescript young man in a scruffy off-the-peg suit, awkward and somehow furtive in his movements. He walked in off the street, without warning or fanfare, and loitered in the reception area for an hour before approaching the desk. In our offices, that meant we had been watching him very carefully for fifty-six minutes.

He sidled up to the low marble-topped desk, looking quickly about to ensure no-one was nearby. When the receptionist turned her warm smile on him, he blushed scarlet to the roots of his conservatively cut blond hair.

"I'd like to speak to Daniel Marsh, please."

The sheer unlikelihood of that request actually caused Jennifer, our receptionist, to momentarily lose her calm face, but she recovered quickly, distracting Lathan with her finest 'you interest me' look while she pressed the panic button with her toe.

For poor Lathan, knowing him like I do now, enduring the following minute must have taken all his willpower to prevent himself curling into a ball on the floor. Security screens crashed down and six heavily armoured men surrounded him, their submachine guns steady: aimed at his head and torso.

"Sir, I am going to ask you to place your bag on the floor and step away from it. If you do not comply, we will shoot you."

Lathan didn't move. Jennifer saved his life by smiling warmly as she said: "Put it down, sir. You know we have to be careful."

He put the bag down and was promptly felled by over four hundred pounds of security guards. When they climbed off, he was unconscious. No undue force had been used; Lathan was simply not a physically robust young man.

An hour later, I knew more about Lathan than his late family had. The searches we can run are extensive and invasive. For obvious reasons, we are not bound by privacy laws, data protection or bureaucratic divisions. What we want, we get.

Lathan Alexander Dove, son of William and Mary Dove, both former professors at Oxford. He was an exceptional student, a loner with few friends, and had had no steady partners of either gender. He held degrees in several areas of science and computing, and could have been working for us, but his mother had some odd history in her twenties. Until a year before his arrival, he had been programming in the City, turning his brilliant mind toward making rich people richer. Then his father committed suicide, after killing his mother. Lathan resigned, spent six months sorting out their estate, then disappeared completely. The sort of off-the-grid that makes normal security agencies worry, and makes us positively paranoid.

It is a bigger, scarier world out there than many realise, and it terrifies me that we do not have the resources to be the omniscient protectors of humanity that we need to be. Our particular Pandora's Box was opened a long time ago, and we can only fight the results that we detect or deduce. All we can do for the rest is pray.

While a couple of nursing staff made sure Lathan was unharmed and comfortable, I made a couple of calls to some people who had the means to track some of those who dropped off the grid. It took eighteen minutes for one of them to come back to me with a single sentence: "He bought Gathern's copy."

My off hand was pressing the 'lockdown' button as I returned the mobile to my pocket. Young Mister Dove had just become a confirmed threat. Whether to us, or only to himself, was all that remained to be determined.

Lathan came round an hour later. He sat up on the low bench and surveyed the small room he was in: the toilet in the corner, the chair, and the door without any visible handle. He nodded, looked up at the camera, and said: "I can remove the play from the 'net."

We had a crisis meeting. Never in our brief history, and never before in the records of all the organisations that preceded us, had this happened: an owner of the play coming forward willingly - and apparently sane. We discussed every scenario, even the ones beyond the daily insanity we knew brooded just beyond the reality we live in. I think we might still have been discussing what to do with Lathan Dove, but someone had other ideas. Jennifer went in with fish and chips for two, along with a couple of mugs of tea. I was in the midst of something highly theoretical – and, quite frankly, unlikely - when our duty sergeant crashed into the room.

"Jennifer's having dinner with him!"

The minutes state that the meeting adjourned swiftly to allow remedial actions to take place. Actually, it fell apart in a chaos of people shouting and running for the door. None of them made it before me, and my heavy-handed 'queue jumping' left two of them needing medical attention. Jennifer is my daughter.

A short time later, I was watching Lathan and Jennifer getting along like two young, smart people who don't get out much sometimes do. My belovedly annoying daughter had even switched the feed to visual-only. I was considering ways to justify an extrajudicial shooting when Jennifer raised the remote that activated the audio and looked over her shoulder at the camera.

"Don't you dare. I'll be out in a bit and then you can shout at me, but I'm not leaving until you stop trying to massage the rules so you can have Lathan suppressed."

Lathan smiled: "'Suppressed' as in 'killed'?"

Jennifer nodded. I heard Lathan say "Oh", before Jennifer switched the audio off again.

I cannot fathom how she knows when I'm watching, but she does. It usually happens when the situation is of importance to one or both of us. So I went and got myself a coffee and made my apologies to those I had mowed down on the way out of the meeting.

By the time I got back to the control room, Jennifer was sitting quietly off to one side, a security guard lingering nearby. I waved him away. She looked at me, noting that my knuckles were white where I gripped the steaming mug.

"Dad, you need to relax. Take a deep breath."

I gave her my sternest stare. She smiled. Daughters: who can defend against them? I eased off a bit, and she nodded.

"Lathan is not influenced. He is fixated, but not where you think. Come and talk to him."

For all my parental-reflex reactions, Jennifer worked with me because she's very good at reading people. If she vouched for Mister Dove's state of mind, I had no real evidence, bar over-protectiveness, to doubt her.

Out of deference to Jennifer, I had Lathan brought to one of our meeting rooms. It was the one with guard positions concealed in the walls, but she didn't need to know that.

Lathan entered, after holding the door open for Jennifer, then sat in the chair furthest from me. Jennifer sat between us: "Anyone for tennis?" she quipped, looking back and forth. I shook my head and moved down the table. Lathan stayed put.

"Mister Dove. Let me be clear. You are a cause of great concern to everyone in this building, except this young lady. Please, do your best to change that."

Lathan nodded: "I'll need my bag. With all of its contents."

I raised my hand and, within a couple of minutes, a security guard silently entered, handed Lathan his bag, and exited swiftly.

Lathan rummaged about for a while, seemingly confirming that all was present and correct. Then he turned his attention fully to me. His gaze was steely. I recognised it as something similar to those I had seen in men returning from the wars in Afghanistan.

"Mister Marsh, I presume. Or, at least, he is probably listening by now. I shall start at the beginning so you can get the full picture."

He hunched forward and picked a single strip of torn paper from his bag. The paper was yellowed with age, and he held it almost tentatively.

"This scrap is all that is left of what I believe to be a full transcription of the play, made by one of my father's students, Ellery Grant."

I knew that, in the control room above, that name was being investigated.

"He's dead. You can tell your people to ease off."

Observant or informed? I wondered.

"As you know by now, my father was a brilliant psychologist, specialising in autosuggestion and induced states of mind. Ellery approached him because he had discovered what he considered to be proof that certain occult writings could induce detrimental states in the reader. Furthermore, he proposed that a group of readers in an induced mental state could exert an influence over certain aspects of what we call reality, in a scaled application similar to that of observing quantum events."

A good thing Mister Grant was dead. It saved me having to order him suppressed.

"My father was sceptical: a state he achieved with ease, I might add. He tasked Ellery with providing a paper to formally quantify his thesis, along with the usual proofs."

Lathan paused to take a sip of water, his need to gather himself obvious to both Jennifer and I.

"Three weeks later, my father returned from a week's sabbatical to find a large treatise on his desk. Ellery could not be found. Unbeknownst to us at the time, he was already dead. His remains were discovered in the wreckage of his camper van, on one of the rarely used side roads that overlook Loch Ness, a few weeks later."

Lathan reached into his bag and pulled out a sheaf of torn paper: quality vellum, by the look of it. The lower edges were singed. "These few pages are all that remain of my father's daybook entries, from the day after the treatise arrived, to the day he committed suicide. It was a loose-leaf notepad-cum-diary. Keeping it was a habit from his youth, and one he maintained religiously. On these pages he made notes and also wrote down extracts."

I straightened up. Extracts of what? Lathan saw my increased attention.

"Yes, they were extracts from the play. From the first act. But what got me was the fragmentary note that survived on the last page."

Lathan held the note toward the camera before holding it high in front of him. He squinted slightly to read the cramped handwriting.

"The main part of the note on the page is lost, but what survives is: 'PTSD slash Somme et al, question mark. Must see original. Find Maxwell Gathern.'"

I could almost hear people upstairs dropping things in shock. What a concept! I decided to move things along.

"You say that's the last page? What happened?"

Lathan looked at me. He refilled his glass and drank it. To my surprise, Jennifer took his hand.

He sighed: "I am not sure of the timing. As far as I can tell, my father threw all his work on the treatise, and the treatise itself, into the fire haphazardly. Some books and documents he threw in whole, some he tore up, some he shredded. But everything went into the fire in his study. Then he went downstairs, twisted and knotted together two of my mother's silk scarves, Thuggee-style, and stalked my mother through the house after she saw him coming and ran. Eventually, he knocked her down the stairs and strangled her in the hall, leaving her hung from the banister. Then he left the house, walked to his car, and siphoned the fuel tank all over himself. He struck the matches just as I returned home. The blast knocked me down. I thought it was an accident, ran to the car and, seeing dad was beyond reach, ran into the house to get mum. I found her in the hall and I am told I put out the fire in the study before it could destroy the house, but I have no memory of that. From seeing mum hanging to coming round in hospital, a week later, is a complete blank."

I slightly regretted moving things along, as Lathan seemed to withdraw into himself. Jennifer leaned close to him whilst pointing toward the door with the hand he couldn't see. Knowing the guards would protect her, I left.

A little while later, Jennifer called me back to the meeting room. Lathan had composed himself, and the table was strewn with bits of paper. He looked up, hesitating momentarily, before he carefully placed a last piece in a corner, away from the rest.

"This is everything I could salvage from my father's notes. I should point out at this point that I am under treatment for post-traumatic stress, but not taking the medication. If I get better, I'll be as susceptible as the usual victims of the play."

Good gods. He knew.

"The stress induced by seeing my parents dead, and knowing why, has induced a disassociation in my mind. That disassociation, I am told, will be detrimental to me. But until I have to have it alleviated, I would like to work with you. I can help, and I am about the only person who can. You have a serious problem that I think you haven't spotted yet."

I raised an eyebrow: "Really?"

Lathan sat down and stared at the ceiling for a while. The silence stretched. Finally, he clapped his hands and looked straight at me.

"What do you know about Carcosa Servers?"

My expression must have told him of my total ignorance.

"I am a programmer by inclination and trade. With a little more amorality and less respect, I'd be a hacker. As it is, I like exploring the World Wide Web, both open and dark sides. I have the skills to get to places where I am not exactly welcome, and to remain undetected. It was on one of those excursions that I found some data which contained familiar prose."

Any icy finger of premonition stroked leisurely down my spine.

"There are people out there who consider the play to be the only way to change the world. They view it as some sort of 'reset'. Bring down the governments, the corrupt, and the ultra-wealthy by caving in their minds. The fact that no-one is immune, and only a few can withstand the effects of the play for any length of time, is irrelevant to them. That those who can withstand the effects have to be suffering some form of dissociative psychosis, is also ignored; if they even care."

The icy finger curled back into the chill fist that twisted my guts.

"The one thing they have in common is organisation. They're distributed, encrypted, stealth-moded, and backed up to hell and gone. You could spend the next ten years blowing up server farms, and they'd end the decade with more servers than when they started. The self-orbiting satellite initiatives open up entire vistas of untouchable madness."

Jennifer raised her hand: "But how will they deliver it?"

Lathan grinned: "Ever heard of things 'going viral'? Well, that's how I'd do it. Make the play something people want to see. Make it a thing of mystery. Rely on the international accords, that I guess are already in place, to ensure that the play achieves the notoriety of censorship. The rest is just waiting. Victims will fall, and those initially unaffected will join. Exponential spread of induced psychoses, with no common symptoms of affliction. My rudimentary calculations predict that it would take a month before being recognised as a problem, by which time it would be unstoppable. The main vectors would be the followers of participating counter-culture and dark 'net 'icons' on social media: more of the 'fashionable' rebels than the actual disaffected. So the greatest impact would be in teenagers and twenty-year olds. They may not bring down civilisation, but they'll certainly cripple two generations at the very least."

My backside hit the seat so hard it rattled my teeth. Lathan didn't let up.

"The nearest scenario I can relate this to would be the Spanish Flu pandemic. Except this will have a vector of anywhere with internet access, no cure, and no drop in lethality."

Jennifer raised her hand again: "Drop in lethality?"

"Pathogenic viruses tend to become less deadly over a period of time, as the hosts of the deadlier strains die off."

I raised a hand: "You are aware that victims of the play do die?"

He nodded: "The number of new readers should offset the losses that would otherwise limit the spread in the way virus fatalities do. In addition, as I had no metrics for those who would suffer deferred onset, I did not include them. Apart from being victims, that group could act as long-term vectors, which only enhances the spread."

I pause in my reflections to park the car. The door behind me opens and closes, without a word being said. I open my thermos, pour a cup, and sip black coffee whilst returning to my memories.

Lathan started working for me that evening. While everyone about was suffering confusion, nausea or closeted denial over his hypotheses, he started gathering a team to work on his proposals. He would not state any of it was definite until he could prove it, and only paused long enough to reassure me that the copy of the play he had obtained from Gathern had been burnt to ashes.

With our computing resources and security clearances, it took him three weeks. It was a bleary-eyed Lathan who placed an inch-thick binder on my desk. I flicked it open and looked up in surprise: the whole thing was hand written. He grinned sheepishly through his exhaustion.

"I don't trust computer security. I know what people like me can do, and I'm not one of the best."

All of my veteran 'hacking' staff disagreed strongly, but Lathan never admitted to his programming genius.

I read his report that night, with Jennifer by my side. She'd come round after settling Lathan down at her place. Which was something else I was not coping at all well with.

The next day, I discussed various aspects of Lathan's single proposal with my information technology teams. All of them agreed that it was theoretically possible. Several of them said that only Lathan, and maybe a dozen other programmers in the world, were capable of doing it. All of them agreed that Lathan could not do it without better information to derive targets from.

So, when Lathan came in with Jennifer after lunch, I endured my daughter's cold, angry stare and handed him what he needed to make his proposal work. It was also the thing that could finish him, but I had no choice.

Lathan looked at the slim binder, reading and rereading the title page. Eventually, he looked up. There were tears in his eyes.

"Where did you get this?" he whispered.

"Your father sent it to Ellery on the morning of the day your parents died."

"Does it have the information I mentioned in my report?"

I looked at Jennifer. Her gaze said a lot of things, none of them good for a father-daughter relationship.

"Yes, Lathan, it does. My people say that it contains a lot more than the minimum you hoped for."

He smiled: "How can you say that?"

I smiled back: "We have scanners. They look for specific words and word-patterns. Even allowing for the limitations of enhanced optical character recognition, they are accurate enough for us to be sure."

Lathan opened the document in the centre and started reading. I reached forward and closed it before he could become engrossed.

"I wouldn't normally say this, but as my daughter is glaring at me like her mother used to when I was about to catch hell, I'll concede this once. Lathan, even if the scanning result is only eighty percent accurate, the report could be as dangerous as the play itself. Your father was brilliant in his analysis and distilled many key aspects: from phrases to common imagery and mood creation. I have no doubt you can get what you need. My people doubt that you will come out untouched, even with the buffer provided by your mental disorder."

Lathan stared at the cover of his father's last treatise. He looked at Jennifer. He looked at me. He looked at the ceiling. Then he did something I never expected. He took Jennifer's hand and turned to look her in the eyes: "With your help, I can do this. There's an outside chance I might even get away with it. Without your help, I can probably do this. But I'm certain that what remains won't be all of me. Either way, I have to do this, because only I can, and I cannot ask for your support."

I watched my daughter cry onto his hands, and wished I could reach back down the centuries to strangle that playwright at birth.

Jennifer nodded: "I'll help."

She turned to me: "I know you had to do this. Please forgive me if I can never forgive you for that."

That was the last time my daughter spoke a whole sentence to me. Over the next six weeks, Lathan went places with programming that left my best scratching their heads. Then he set them to seeding every possible nook and cranny of the world-wide web, and its subsidiaries, which so many of us take for granted, with his carefully designed programs. I got the job of forcing the owners of several major operating systems, and the people behind a large number of security packages, to add some programs to their 'approved' lists, or next releases, and to do so without any testing or documentation. I got a lot older during those few weeks.

Jennifer spent all her time with Lathan. The people I had tasked with observing said that she seemed to calm him, to be able to bring him back from the contemplative silences he fell into: ones that glazed his eyes with increasing frequency.

Five months, two weeks and six days after Lathan started, I got a call in the dead of night. Lathan had been taken to hospital. Jennifer had left a DVD with one of my special operatives, with instructions to place it directly into my hands. I got dressed and went to the office. The DVD was handed over, and the operative was stationed outside my door, before I pressed 'play'.

The scene was Jennifer's bedroom. Lathan was sitting in bed with books, papers and my daughter's underwear scattered about. Nice touch, Jennifer. From the timestamp, it was about two months after Lathan had started his programming. He looked wild-eyed but more relaxed than I had ever seen him.

"Hold it steady, Jenny. No messing about. Your dad will need this."

At least one person in that bedroom bore no malice.

"Mister Marsh. I'm recording this now, in case I am unable to report in person."

I heard a stifled sniff from the holder of the camera.

"I'll try and leave out the technical bits. You need to know what the beastie I'm writing will do. This program can simplistically be described as a virus designed to do good things. It also has to do them without anyone being aware of what it's up to. So I've put bits of it all over the place, each bit being something that no-one will pay attention to. A little program left over from earlier versions, a ghost of an image remaining from a system tidy up; there is lots of obsolete code lying about on computers. But now, some of it is mine.

My program is made up of a lot of smaller modules, and in a very complex way borrows from two-part explosives. Harmless and untraceable apart, effective together. I thought this was the best way to ensure the program perpetuates. With your inclusion of modules deep in most operating systems and security suites, it should exist as long as the internet runs architecture and software that resembles what we have now. I don't see that changing for a while. Not forever, but long enough for this threat to go quiet. Each complete program is part payload, part defences. Attempts to reverse engineer my work will cause the most amusing things to happen to analysis or editing software. Whatever your definition of amusing, the end result is that I am happy that my stuff will be considered too much trouble when there are so many other programs out there to hack."

Lathan paused and waved at Jennifer: "Back in a bit." The screen went black. A moment later, it returned, the timestamp having moved on an hour.

"What the program does is as I laid out in my proposal. It searches computer files for traces of the play. It can penetrate virtually every file type out there. The ones it can't, I have listed in the documentation, and you'll have to find a way to access them so my program can do its stuff. What it does when it finds a copy, or part, of the play is the tricky bit. It doesn't destroy anything. It replaces. It substitutes words, it swaps out phrases. The end result is the play, but with the trigger points removed. It's still disturbing, but only on a par with classic weird fantasy. What I aimed for was to shred the dangerous elements, to defuse it, but without letting anyone know it has been messed with. That way interest will wane and the play should sink from the public eye without fanfare, in the same way that all over-hyped internet crazes do."

He paused to take a sip of water, then grinned: "Of course, read-only media presented a challenge. In the case of a DVD or similar, what is on the media and what is displayed will be slightly different. If my software can censor, it will. If it can't, the media will show as being 'unreadable'."

Lathan gestured with his hand and the camera angle rose, presumably as Jennifer stood up.

"Give me the camera, Jenny. Could you go and get us a snack?"

There were a few moments of chaotic angles, and then darkness. Then the picture returned, and Lathan loomed large in the view.

"Better make this quick. I've finished the program. Tomorrow I start extracting key data from my father's treatise to give the program its targets. I've loaded the substitutions already. The only thing left is typing the extracts of the play in. Then I have to test it. Either way, if you'll excuse my language, I'm expecting to suddenly become badly fucked up sometime in the next few weeks. Jenny doesn't know that it is a certainty, not a possibility. Be ready, she'll need you. Especially if she has to help me hold my mind together for an extended period, while I complete this project. The play turns its victims strange. Too strange for most to handle without scars."

He paused and seemed to consider something for a moment, then nodded to himself and added: "I'm no expert outside of computing, but please consider this layman's opinion: I'm certain that there has to be more to this than just a play." He paused again, then held the camera close: "I couldn't have done what you did, letting your daughter stay with me. Thank you."

He cocked his head.

"She's coming back."

The screen went black for a moment, then he resumed as if he was finishing off a topic that he'd covered while Jennifer was out of the room: "The program will self-replicate and hunt whenever it encounters new systems or files. I predict it will eventually suffer a lot of interference, but hope that the discovery time will be after it has done its work."

A door opened and he looked off screen to his right.

"Oh, that looks good. Take this so I can stretch, then after I finish, we can eat."

The camera angle went off again, before settling back into the original view.

"As I said, the program cannot get everywhere. There is also a chance that some of the smarter system administrators may spot it. Either way, it will not be a clean sweep. It's like an inoculation. It may not be able to get all the places distributing the play, but it's got a high percentage chance of de-fanging copies of the play opened on most computers before the reader can reach the venomous bits. That's where your people come in, Daniel."

He called me Daniel. First and last time ever.

"You will need to police this like you have been, except with a little more attention to net distribution. I've left your teams my scanning programs, and the only copy of the entire program will be added to this disk when I finish, along with the source code."

A cursor flashed and green letters scrolled across the bottom of the screen like a ticker feed:

```
The program and source code are on here. The target
data from my father's treatise has not been
included and I have destroyed the original document
you gave me. You will also find that some of the
test files I used to prove my programs were your
scans of the treatise. Sorry, but the potential for
trying to use this as a weapon is something I
cannot chance, even with you.
```

I smiled with relief when I read that. I was relieved because I wouldn't have had the courage to do it, or to order it done.

"That's it. Anything else would be telling you what you already know. Wish me luck, and good luck to all of you."

Lathan raised a hand in farewell and the screen went blank. I took the disc out of the player, unplugged it, and walked the disc, escorted by the operative who had been outside my office, down to the vault. The disc has not been disturbed since.

I take a swig of coffee and look up at the swooping architecture of the place, lights shining on the rain-slicked stonework. My eyes track without conscious effort to the far window on the second floor, where the corner room benefits from the finest views of dawn across rolling woodland. Up there, Jennifer is reading to Lathan. More correctly, she's reading to what's left of him. He looks the same, except his features seem a little slack, and he's lost weight. But the biggest loss shows in his eyes. He went too far into something mankind should never have set eyes upon, and it kept most of him.

I look at my watch. Another three hours, or thereabouts. She always reads him *Alice in Wonderland*. It calms him, and the staff say that for the few hours while my daughter is reading, he doesn't cry.

Dreaming of Cailida

By night, in dreams, I stood by that lake and watched her from afar. In a dress softened with shades of aged cream, she walked slowly upon a jetty, the muted lights of an indistinct city behind her. Her gait was thoughtful, even pensive. She gazed at the bouquet in her grasp, while wandering a cage defined by the piers of the narrow way.

As a child I saw only the city and a silhouette. In my teens, I lusted after her in an abstract way that I did not understand. When love and marriage befell, I did not see her for years. But as my marriage withered, she returned, and I beheld more of what I imagined to be her plight.

Within the acrimony of my divorce there lay a core of maudlin pleasure, as days of frustration and anger, over the petty things that destroy love, led to nights of clearer vision.

I went from family man to bachelor. My circle of friends closed about my ex-wife, amputating me with an ease that seemed too callous, too precise, to be mere circumstance. I found that I cared less for the loss of fickle company than for the nights when the distractions of the day clouded that lake with mist.

Life, for me, became two dreams, joined only by the acts of drowsing and waking. My work became easy, as the travails that had beset me fell away. Going home was no longer accompanied by the dread of marital confrontation, whilst the vicarious politics and playground animosities that infested my place of work became naught but the susurruses of irrelevant mannequins.

The further I fell into a calm acceptance of the triviality of life, acknowledging the futility of striving against a world set only to distract, the stronger the lake and its environs became. It was as if I alone had woken to the fact that waking, itself, was the antithesis of contentment.

And so there came a night where the winter's cold accompanied a moonless sky, and I settled into repose as soon as I returned from work. With a smile I quaffed my valerian and *verte* absinthe, a concoction I had found to be efficacious in separating me from distractions.

The clearing of the mists, which followed the languor suffusing my body, was accompanied by a rush of warmth. It was something I had never felt before. The tremble in my mind, a stirring of primitive fear, succumbed almost before I could define where the feeling of unease came from. The peace that flowed through my soul, as the vista broadened before me, was exquisite.

Upon that distant shore I stood, under a cavernously dark night sky that was sparsely strewn with stars blacker than the heavens in which they were set - yet perfect in their alignment to laws unwritten.

For the first time, I saw the barren shores to either side of the city across the lake, where the jagged edges of walls gave way to the rounded crenelations of headstones. Outside of those, only a few lonely nubs of stone sat amidst sere grasses.

She was there upon the jetty, but stood for the first time at its furthest point, nearest me and far from any shore. She gazed across the lake, and for a moment my heart thundered; then realisation came that she looked to my left, not to me.

I looked to see what she beheld and, to my surprise, a figure stood near me upon the shore. His pale yellow vestments fell in tatters and loose wrappings, so voluminous and numerous in layers that I could not make out his form or footwear. Upon his head, a high-tined crown of ashen silver rested lightly above a face concealed with a mask of pallid and jaundiced fright. Near-colourless hair whipped about his ears and neck in a wind I did not feel. At my extended regard, the head turned and eyes of the softest grey caught mine.

"Hail to thee who stands upon this shore undaunted." The voice seemed to come from further afield than the motionless lips.

"I have visited this place in dreams my whole life. Always upon this shore, always to regard the woman standing upon yonder jetty."

"It is her fate and yours."

"To watch each other?"

"For her to wait and for you to watch. She is dear Cailida, who is loved from afar."

"Why only from afar?"

"To cross this lake you must quit your dream."

"My dream? This is my dream."

Flecks of gold spun in his eyes as he smiled, then smiled wider at my shocked expression. The stars above shuddered, shifted, and my illusion broke.

"Will you introduce us?"

His head turned and the distant voice whispered: "It would be fitting. Accompany me."

In my mind's eye I saw a sleeping body sprawled across a floor, stains of terror stark against torn sheets dragged from a bed gone cold. Thankfully, that horrific vision faded as he led me across the lake, with stars above and stars below, toward a jetty where my lady had waited for so long.

Turning my head, I looked back to see a row of figures upon the shore that we had quit. Each reached a hand in slow denial, either toward me, or to cover their eyes.

Black Country Prodigal

I was born and raised in the industrial heart of England, hating every moment of the monotonous grind that everyone about me took to be their lot. The Great War had opened up society at last, yet here we were: still grubbing in the dirt for our stipend.

The grime and the poverty were almost bearable until an owner would come past, his carriage or car shining, his shirt snowy white, and his companions all arrayed in pristine dress. All of them with clean hands, because they had never needed to grind the muck into their skin to earn a living.

It was intolerable. From flat-capped tearaway to frustrated artist was simply the next step for me. I toyed with gambling and sundry other ways to pay for my comforts, but all I was doing was circling the pits that my family had served for generations. Coal was gold in these hills. Men who owned it, or clawed it from the ground by hand and pick, had money. Those who did not could only get money from those who worked coal in some way.

In this manner, it was not very long before my parents called in our family's one successful member to rein in my recalcitrant ways.

Uncle Thomas was a big man, drawn from quarry-worker stock and made sharp by going from pick-man to owner by his own sweat and craft. I thought he would understand. He did, but not in any way that shed sympathy upon my rebellious dreams.

I stood in the tiny dining room of our home as mother harried the family out, so he and I could talk without prying ears and sarcastic sniping from my siblings. As the door closed, Uncle Thomas looked about at the threadbare furnishings and chipped best crockery, still proudly displayed upon the dresser.

"Your folks have had a hard time of it, Nat. They were looking to you to improve their lot. To say you've been a disappointment is an understatement. What's your problem, lad?"

I waved my hand at the room and the window, out toward the terraces outside and the colliery beyond: "All of this. I cannot stand it. My soul cries for finer fare: to write poetry and read books, to mix with free-thinkers and jovial company. Not dour-faced miners who work alongside their fathers and grandfathers, who consider the pianist at The Lurcher to be somehow effete, no matter that he worked alongside them until a collapse ruined his leg."

His eyes widened in surprise: "Well, that's not what I heard. I heard you were just another shiftless wastrel who ruined your family's standing in these parts with your selfish ways. It seems they have it all wrong."

I smiled. At last, someone who grasped my rueful situation.

Uncle Thomas' brows lowered: "You're no wastrel. You're a damn fool, and a feckless one at that. Dreams and airs are no substitute for hard work. If you want finery and pretty words, you can do your time on the land, like I did. Earn your leisure! Shake the thoughts of being some nonny word-monger from your addled head, lad. There's none from these parts who have a damn thing to offer the arts. We're working men and we do it well. So would you, if you'd only buckle down to it."

His words rocked me back, his expression stalling any hope of being understood. It finally became crystal clear: there was nobody here who had the vision to see what I needed.

Uncle Thomas patted me affably on the shoulder: "Come see me tomorrow, Nat. I've got a couple of positions going and you can pick the one that appeals to you."

With that, he left. Obviously, in his mind, the situation was resolved. The would-be prodigal had been returned to the fold with stern words from a successful man of the land.

I crept from the house late that night, and blundered my way to the railway station in time for the first train of the day. The takings from my father's pot of ale money got me a single to Coventry. I was headed south, away from the drudgery and the terraces. Headed for somewhere I could realise my aspirations and, of course, have people recognise in me the greatness that was surely my due.

Coventry was the biggest place I had ever seen, and it didn't take me long to find my way down to the colourful side of town. Having money and leisure got me friends right quick, until the money ran out. But my long-frustrated talent for word-crafting blossomed, and I soon found myself sharing a room with Bessy Grey, a young woman who worked in the textile mills. The house was a chaos of textile girls and their beaus, with diversions available at all hours.

Bessy loved my poetry and near-swooned into my arms when I composed pieces about her, much to the amusement of her friends. We didn't have much, but she said that an artist like me should be free of such considerations. She would happily work to support me, until I achieved the recognition I deserved.

That was all well and good, but my luck at cards took a turn for the worst, so Bessy took to working longer at the mill to keep a roof over our heads. Which left me free to linger in the artist's state of mind even more. Composition of new works led, of course, to the requirement for performing them. My audience was limited, but I found one Rose Turner to be a rapt listener. With Betty away, Rose took to entertaining me in return for my composing verses about her.

When Betty found out about Rose, she confronted her 'rival' and they proceeded to hiss and spit like angry cats. When their anger turned to fighting, I made myself scarce - after emptying their purses while everyone else was watching them claw at each other. Coventry plainly did not have the right atmosphere for my talent to flourish in.

At the station, the women's meagre coinage only got me a single to Northampton. So be it! My muse was calling me further afield. I would obey.

Northampton was like Coventry, except for being marginally cleaner. My year in Coventry had inured me against the mistakes I had made upon arriving there. No sleeping rough this time. I took up with some lads from the shoe factories and through them, made the acquaintance of Lizzie Bunton. Her winsome smile captivated me and spurred my creative side, especially when I found out that whispered recitals of intimate verse made her abandon all restraint.

Within two weeks of arriving, I had moved in with Lizzie at the house she shared with her brother, Alf. With their parents and grandparents gone, Alf was somewhat over-protective of Lizzie. This I discovered, when he and a couple of his cronies gave me a beating, the first evening I ventured out onto the streets while Lizzie was at work.

"You take your fancy words and leave my sister alone." That sentence was the only one he ever uttered to me. He may well have had more, but the following night I ambushed him as he returned from the pub, sotted and staggering. I took everything he had in his pockets. Keeping his money, I dropped everything else into a cesspit, along with the bloodied knife I had taken from a sleeping drunk on my way to Coventry railway station. He would become nothing but another unfortunate victim of callous fate and desperate times.

Lizzie was beside herself, but I calmed her with fine words and an understanding shoulder. Alf's mates gave me evil looks, but none stepped up to accuse me of what they suspected. For half a year I lodged at Lizzie's, even gaining a measure of acceptance from Alf's mates. I was always good for a juicy tale or some racy doggerel, and never folded a game without letting them win a little back.

Then came the day that little Millicent Chambers fell into the same cesspit where I had tossed the non-monetary contents of Alf's pockets. They had to seek her body using billhooks and grapnels. One of those grapnels came back with Alf's pocket watch, - a family heirloom - its chain tangled around my knife. Lizzie would recognise both, without a doubt.

I had been passing by, fortunately hidden from the scene by a fence. By the time the hue and cry went up, I was better than halfway to the station. My muse was calling me to London at last.

London was awful. Filled with ne'er-do-wells and failed poets. After I had gotten my bearings and taken several beatings, I realised that everyone there - or at least those at any level which would afford me the trappings necessary for my comfort and inspiration - had someone watching over them,. With that, I realised that London would not be to me as it had been to Wilde: where his greatest works had been penned.

It took me but a night to take, from folk inattentive of their money, the wherewithal to decamp once more. My muse had called me southward and I had foolishly thought she meant London. Oh, that she could speak plain. It would have saved me so much time.

But then again, maybe my travails were necessary. I had hardly been a man of the world when I left home. The artist within must be fed fortune both fair and foul, must experience the heights and the troughs that life has to offer. I had plainly not been ready. Now I was. Brighton would see to the nurturing and burgeoning of my gift.

The seaside was a revelation to me: the vast expanse of the English Channel spellbinding, by sunlight or moonlight. I found a transient society of rich folk on holiday or taking some vague medical 'cure', all of whom were desperately seeking diversion. A young man with the gift of poetry and a northern accent was something of note. I settled in quickly, and soon accrued all the trappings I required: from velvet smoking jacket to garret accommodation with a window that looked out over views of the sea.

My circle of admirers grew as I obtained a reputation, both for poetry and being able to 'handle myself', as the local lads put it. I went from soirée to bordello via gentleman's club and backstreet den, revelling in every moment. I had quills and inks to scribe for every mood, and my muse and I were productive.

Not so hale were my attempts to get published. The presses were run by mean-spirited men; for all that they claimed to be beset night and day by vagabonds claiming to be the reincarnation of Wilde himself.

So I bided my time and wrote ever more, whilst selecting my dalliances with care for their looks, wealth, and the temporary nature of their residency.

After two years, I found the lake of creativity had drained to be nought but a lacuna. Frustration took me on ever wilder courses in search of inspiration, and I ventured from well-trodden haunts into the fraught underworld of intoxicants, deviancies and one-night dalliances. The nature of those who inhabited this substrate of polite society was mercurial and deliberately ambiguous. After experimenting with the downfalls of many great artists, and even the carnal recreations espoused by Wilde, I moved on. I was disenchanted with physical stimulus. My soul needed satiation, not my body. After a summer of debauching the flesh, I was determined to debase my mind. In that, it seemed that Brighton finally opened its secret heart to me and I plunged in, coming to rest in the arms of the dissolute sister of the infamous green fairy.

Absinthe adulterai was her name, and in her I found my muse transformed to speak in visions of wonder. Ceilings became windows onto spiralling vistas of colour and emotions too fine to be discerned amidst the coarse concerns of the day. In this manner, I whiled away the year and a fair part of the following spring.

It was on a Monday morning that I sat upon the beach, watching the waves roll in, while the sea air cleared the last vestiges of my weekend's diversions from my mind. I was just considering the problem of obtaining a substantial, rather than adequate, breakfast when my eyes were drawn to a vision of beauty strolling along the beach. She walked barefoot upon the sand, betwixt tide and stone, her movements fluid with unconscious grace. A delicate parasol sheltered the perfect complexion of an English rose from the harsh ministrations of the sun. Auburn hair floated and curled on the breeze as green eyes moved lazily, watching her companion, a Golden Retriever, play in the surf. As she hastily brought her parasol down, to save herself from the dog's vigorous shaking off of water, our eyes met. It was like a voltage passed between her soul and mine. Without apparent conscious thought, she stepped toward me, and I rose to step rapidly down onto the sand, so that her feet would not be bruised by crossing the stones to where I sat.

She smiled as I cut a rakish bow: "You are the northern poet, are you not? Nathaniel?"

I matched her smile with one of my own as I took her hand and touched my lips to it, never taking my gaze from hers.

"I am honoured beyond measure to be remembered by such beauty." I released her hand. She did not lower it immediately.

"Emma Fellowes spoke quite effusively of your attentions, Nathaniel."

As well she may have. Her month-long sojourn had been lively, both in and out of clothing.

"How is dear Emma?" I deadpanned.

Her smile told me that she had received all of the details.

"She is betrothed and soon to be married. One could even say with unseemly haste. Rumours hint at her being with child. Wilder rumours whisper that her fiancé is not the father."

"I am sure that such improprieties are but idle chatter. She was the very spirit of virtue and vivacity on the occasions that I saw her. Please, call me Nat."

Her smile transformed into a wicked grin: "Very well, Nat. You may call me Cecily. My four-legged friend is Sebastian. We will be here for a while - I have been prescribed the sea air. As I have never been to Brighton before, could I avail myself of your knowledge of town and society in the same way that Emma did?"

"It would be my pleasure." I bowed again.

"To please me," she whispered.

I kept my composure and did not stumble to the ground. She smiled as I straightened up, and took my arm when proffered.

"You look like a man in need of a decent breakfast."

Her perceptive comment made me stare, as it had been my all-consuming thought at the moment I had set eyes upon her. But her laughter upon seeing my startlement removed all strangeness from the coincidence. With a mutual lightness of step, we proceeded to quit the beach. At her side trotted Sebastian, tongue lolling and sun-dried spume scattering his pale coat with flecks of white. I hoped that my preferred tearooms did not object to canine companions, for I had a hunger to assuage and I guessed that Cecily was not short the means or the willingness to cover the bill.

For all that we inspired a mutual ardour in each other, Cecily was not wont to be bedded that day, or even during the following month. In a transport of delight underpinned by dreaming lust, I excelled myself at finding every soirée, repertory and society ball into which I could inveigle myself and my beauteous companion.

Her insistence that Sebastian accompany her everywhere was at first strange, but her winning smile and warm manner always won me over. That winsome way also allowed Sebastian ingress to places that I could have sworn would have denied even royalty the company of a pet.

A month became two and, while we talked intimately about our lives and aspirations, she still did not give way to needs that we both felt. For me, it was frustration incarnate, as I had not felt such a burning desire for anything except my particular cocktail of *la muse verte* for over a year. For her it was, at first, more difficult to say. She had obviously known men, and had known them well, from what she revealed in conversation. But, although we exchanged many passionate *baiser amoureux*, she would not countenance the slightest intimacy beyond that. When I tasked her about it one night, she muttered something about 'upsetting Sebastian'. I guessed that to be an evasion to conceal pain, and resolved to let the matter rest. We got on so well, and maybe, with time, the pain would fade and she would lose her reticence.

It was a month later that she hinted about trying absinthe. I had discussed my liquid muse, and read her my poems, on several occasions. Given that my state of grace - concerning the pleasures of the flesh and the benefits of celibacy - was not sitting well with me, it was with motives both pure and lascivious that I agreed to share my muse with her.

The following night set in clear and warm. I lit candles in my attic abode, scattered cushions and pillows about, and draped cloths or shirts over the less agreeable aspects of the décor. Cecily arrived and looked about with a knowing smile, while Sebastian moved, without hesitation, to curl himself upon the venerable rug in the centre of the room.

I offered her a choice of either a chair at the table or the armchair behind the door, but she chose to sit herself upon the bed, moving deliberately to put a decorous distance between us as I poured sizeable measures of absinthe into goblets. We shared a pipe of Sir Walter Raleigh Smoking Tobacco; a pleasure Cecily had introduced me to - much to my surprise. Then, with a certain trepidation, we sipped the green liquid and fell to conversation that started with the usual after-dinner topics. It was like we had just met. As goblets emptied, as if of their own accord, our conversation took off for heights that I knew I would not remember, for all that I wished to.

We shared laughter and tears, exchanged secrets and embarrassments. I wrought free verse on the spot until she begged for mercy. Refilled goblets were reaching half-empty, when my ease and the candour of our discussions caused me to reveal the less laudable moments of my trip from colliery town to seaside. After listening in horror, as the tale of Alf tripped from my lips with unconscious candour, I waited with aching heart for Cecily to retreat in disgust.

To my utter confounding, she barely blinked. I watched a single, sapphire-yellow, tear roll from her eye, down her cheek and along her jawline, to fall from her chin. It splashed lightly upon her breast and rolled out of sight into the shadows of her cleavage.

"We both have darknesses within, Nat. Now I know the real you, let us end this charade of reserve."

Without further ado she got up, slipped herself from her dress and stood naked except for stockings and garter belt. My breath caught and then I folded over in agony as my burgeoning, rampant desire tangled in my underwear. Cecily howled with laughter much throatier than I had ever heard from her, before moving to assist me out of my clothes and into her.

Our joining was a thing of heat and light, where our absinthe-enhanced and lust-enflamed senses added almost unendurable pleasure, to the point of agony, combined with searing visions. For me, it was as if the merest touch of her flesh was drawn in sheets of colour and showers of fire; whereas my slightest easing caused barrages of icy blue crystals to rain across my sight and chills to race along my flanks.

We rode each other to heavens beyond endurance, and then took ourselves higher, until ecstasy and inebriation sent us down into the velvet darks of satiated, exhausted sleep.

I rolled over, and a stabbing pain in my side accompanied a dry cracking beneath me. Starting awake in the grey of pre-dawn, I could not make out what I had rolled upon. I slid over the edge of the bed and fumbled for the candle in the dish that I left beneath. Before I found it, I encountered old, folded paper and pulled that out of the way.

Having retrieved the candle, I lit it with shaking hands and turned to stand naked, proud and smiling, before Cecily. The light fell on the bed and I beheld bones. Bones that poked through, or extended from, a torn and stained nightgown of delicate weave, turned yellow with age. The skull upon the pillow fell to one side as I watched, revealing a few brittle fragments of hair with the slightest hints of auburn against the off-white pillowcase.

Aghast, I turned to Sebastian. Upon the moth-eaten rug there curled the desiccated corpse of a dog. Mercifully, the candle was extinguished, in its fall from my palsied hand, as I fainted dead away.

The light of a bright and cheery summer afternoon filled the room when I awoke. There was no change in the horror. A dead dog on my rug and a crushed corpse in my bed: a skeleton garbed in a rotted negligee that displayed the dried stains of my ardour.

I vomited the contents of my stomach into my washing bowl, then opened the window wide and took great, shuddering breaths. When my hands no longer quivered at the end of outstretched arms, I turned to view the room and take stock. My eye fell upon the paper I had retrieved from under the bed. I moved from the window to let the sunlight illumine the room, and, keeping my eyes averted from bed and rug, picked up the paper. It was a Brighton Gazette, dated 13th November 1890. Upon perusing the crackling pages, I decided that local papers had not changed much in the decades since it had been printed. I was about to cast it aside when a small sketch on the second page caught my eye. Under it was a single paragraph:

Heiress Presumed Dead

Cecelia O'Hagan is now considered to have met with foul play at the hands of person or persons unknown whilst on a weekend trip to Brighton. She and her constant companion, a Golden Retriever named Sebastian, disappeared a year ago this week. In all that time, there have been no sightings or any attempts made to gain ransom or reward. The police, with the agreement of her family, today announced this sad conclusion to their search.

The sketch was a fair rendition of Cecily. I sat until tears stained the page and the setting sun's light turned the room golden. I could not help myself, I looked again. What I suspected to have somehow been Cecily remained a partially crushed skeleton upon the bed.

I turned and stared at the carcass on the rug until I could take no more, then crossed to the table and downed the entire, barely touched second bottle of absinthe without taking a breath. Hesitating not one whit, I wadded and smoked a pipe full of Sir Walter's best as fast as my chest would let me.

As the room shook like a leaf in the wind, I steadied myself against the door. There was a mystery here, and if Wilde's green fairy and intrepid Sir Walter's finest could not lead me to the truth, I knew that I was doomed to madness. As it was, my rent was paid some months in advance; I had ample time to separate solution from impossibility.

I shook my fist in defiance at whatever malevolence beset me: "I have time, d'you hear me? I have time!"

"Time" said Sebastian's corpse, "is of no consequence."

I stared at it, convinced of my final descent into bedlam.

The mummified Golden Retriever continued: "But in truth, nor is form, or place."

The garret became a parlour, and I saw a matriarch in rich afternoon dress pause her sipping from an exquisite bone china cup to regard me with puzzlement.

"Just visiting." I stammered. She dropped her cup, and its impact upon the carpet shattered everything about me like glass. Except for the deathly canine, which hung next to me in the all-encompassing inky blackness that the fragmentation had revealed.

The undead dog turned to face me, assuming a sitting position: "Cecily wandered far and found a home. But she was so desperate for a match that, in a moment of maudlin weakness, I allowed her a sojourn. She thought she had found shelter for her soul in you. I had only to wait for your true nature to rape that delusion and, in so doing, send her back."

I looked about frantically, but dark was all about us: "What?"

Sebastian cocked his head: "You are a charlatan, Nathaniel."

"I am a poet."

"I have seen many poets. You are barely competent. Your charlatanry is in your pretence of otherworldliness while you lie, cheat, steal, and murder to maintain your delusions."

"How would you know?"

"I did not, until you told all to her. A man speaking is like an open book. Every nuance of breath and flesh, every flicker of eye and twitch of hand. When the story your body told is combined with your words, truth did out. You are a charlatan."

"I am a poet. A visionary poet at that. Fantastic realms are my domain."

"Could you prove that to our satisfaction?"

"Cecily lives?"

"Not as crass flesh of earth and water. As I said, she went home. There, she is manifest."

"Then I will prove you wrong." I had no idea what I was accepting, but absinthe and smoke fed raging denial over wounded pride. Let this phantom do its worst. I would not fail.

The darkness poured away like water running off a longshoreman's sou'wester. I stood upon a barren shore, skeletal trees at my back and a lake like smoked glass before me. Across that lake a city shone with lights the colour of Cecily's single tear.

"Take my hand. We shall cross."

I turned to behold a figure in tattered yellow robes, his face obscured by a voluminous hood that rose crookedly to a rounded point nearly an arm's length behind him. He extended a pallid hand with grey nails that were webbed with black cracks: each like a tiny, broken pane of glass.

"Look yonder."

Upon a jetty, which ran from the foot of the city far out into the lake, a familiar figure stood.

"Cecily." I took the hand. His touch was like cold fire, but I gritted my teeth and endured.

When he stepped out onto the surface of the lake, I quailed, then long-stepped to keep pace, before my hesitation drew his attention. We walked upon the inky water as if it were nought but a parquet floor, and I saw stars reflected in it. Looking up, I saw two moons hurtle by, under a sky so dark I wondered how I could still see the black stars, scattered like lumps of coal upon a sandy beach.

Midway across, he stopped. I stopped.

"This is the place. Gaze upon me and accept your place in this place."

First, I looked at Cecily and thought of nights spent wenching and gambling whilst swilling liquor. I felt icy liquid run into my shoes.

"You seem shorter." There was amusement in his tone.

My rage rekindled and I stared him in the pits he had for eyes, the mask he wore making them seem to be set impossibly far back in his head. I saw golden flecks whirl in orbs of grey, deep within sockets like melted wax, and wanted to down a tankard of ale in The Lurcher. Water rose, or I sank, and my ankles started to go numb.

"Definitely shorter."

"I. Am. No. Charlatan." The words came with great difficulty. The cold had raced from my feet to my gut. I felt my manhood shrivel.

He moved his head closer and the mask curved into a hideous smile. I tasted wormwood and smelt my own excrement, then turned and screamed vomit into the lake as I went under. Cold, beyond anything I had ever felt, smote me like a hammer. I welcomed the darkness that took me away.

I awoke, shivering, in that place of inky blackness.

The mummified dog had yellow eyes. Odd how I hadn't remarked upon that before.

The bony tail wagged slowly: "Shall we continue, or has your desire for otherworldliness ebbed somewhat?"

I dredged my soul for words and, finding none, croaked forth: "Ebbed."

The dog shook itself, and the darkness was shot with streaks of gold.

"Then away with you, ghost of rebellion. Back to your tainted absinthe and affectation of ennui, to your vacuous poetry and hollow lamentations."

The darkness collapsed, like viewing a balloon deflating from within. I found myself sat in the armchair of my garret room, with only two mouldering corpses for company.

I curled myself into the tightest ball I could manage and sobbed. Tomorrow I would send a telegram to my uncle, and tell him that he had been right in his opinion of me. Then I would walk south until blue water filled the abysm where my lies had been.

HOUSE OF SORROWS

Mum said that dad finished reading the play at three in the morning, on the day after my twenty-second birthday. I was in Iraq. They had chatted with me by video link the previous evening. None of us had any warning - he just read it, and faded away. What was left looked like my dad, except for the eyes: they were empty. He had possessed an erudition that never ceased to astound me – yet all that remained was a husk that looked like my father.

After the initial therapy, he cleaned floors at a local supermarket: part of the continuing attempt to retrieve his mind from wherever it had gone. He could take care of himself and was safe to be let out - after he learned which bodily functions could be done in public, and which ones had to be attended to in the men's room.

Someone had to drive him there each morning and collect him each evening. When he was brought home, he sat in his old armchair in the lounge and someone had to switch the television to the BBC twenty-four-hour news channel. Somewhere between two and four hours later, he would move from the chair to the corner of the room and curl up on a woollen blanket. We had put it there after it became clear that going upstairs was something he would not do, and after any form of bed in that corner had been rejected as well.

In the morning he would wake, go to the bathroom, strip, wash and then put on the fresh clothes left out, or don the previous day's, if there weren't any. He would be standing in the hall, waiting, by the time whoever was driving him was ready to leave. That was his entirety. If you said "day off", he would return to sit in front of the television and wait for someone to switch it to the BBC. If the channel was not changed, he uttered the only sound he ever made after the reading: a mournful, heart-rending wail of inconsolable fear and loss.

He had been wailing for hours before the police broke in. The cable box had failed, sometime after Mum had fallen down the stairs and expired slowly, paralysed and bleeding inside. The last thing she saw would have been him sitting in front of the television.

The police called my sister, and she called me. I came home through winter snow to a bleak house full of people I no longer knew. It took me less than six hours to drive them all away. After that, my sister and I started to rebuild our lives.

Our parents had been affectionate, but distracted by their pursuits. Which caused a distance to grow between us and them. But it brought the two of us closer, and, with this cruel ending of our family, once more it came down to Christina and I to take care of each other.

It was several weeks later when the conversation we had both been avoiding took place. We sat down at the dining table, had a light lunch, and then caught each other's eye. We both knew it was time.

"Can we afford care for him?" She was still a little bleary-eyed from lack of sleep and the occasional bout of crying. I probably didn't look much better.

I gazed from the dining room, across the hall, into the lounge. Dad sat motionless in front of the TV. I ran my gaze up to the ceiling and back down to her face.

"I've had several offers from PMCs." She pursed her lips to indicate a lack of understanding, and I grinned: "Private Military Company. They pay a lot to get people like me. On top of that, we can sell the house."

She looked startled, as if the idea of selling came as a surprise.

"I hadn't considered the house. But I thought that you said you'd never work as a mercenary."

That hit home: "You're right. But needs must and Dad's care has to come before my reservations. Besides, it might be better than I expect."

Chris's reply was unspoken, as we both turned at the sound of a heavy hand pounding on the door.

I touched her shoulder: "You expecting anyone?"

"No."

At that, I moved to the door and latched the double chains, before opening it slowly. Outside was a very nicely dressed young man, brandishing a folder with a garish logo promoting 'Evesham

Property Acquisitions'. As the door reached the limit of the chains, he smiled, revealing dazzlingly white teeth.

"Good morning, Mister Whitecross."

"No-one of that surname here." Because of an old family feud on dad's side, we had both inherited mum's surname.

He barely missed a beat, swiftly glancing at something hidden from my view by the folder, before looking back at me: "So you'd be Mister Lukather Shaw. Is that Miss Christina Shaw I see behind you?"

Our doorstep visitor had just crossed the line from 'harmless annoyance' to 'over-prepared for unknown reasons'. I didn't like his smile, either.

"We could be. Depends on what you're selling."

He waved a hand in a dismissive gesture: "Selling? Good grief, no. I must apologise for arriving so soon after your bereavement, but I have something that is simply too good to wait any longer."

"Really? Who would you be, exactly?"

With an audible 'snap' of cloth, his arm retracted to his pocket, then shot forward with a business card pinched between index and middle finger.

"Andrew Tyler of Evesham Property Acquisitions. We work to link those who wish to buy quickly with those who have properties to sell rapidly." He stepped back and pointedly stared at the chained door.

"You're fine right there. Make your pitch."

He actually winced at my use of the word 'pitch'.

"Well, sir and madam. I represent a gentleman who is looking for an early twentieth century property with decent gardens and views -

in this area. When he saw the coverage of your mother's unfortunate death, we were immediately engaged to make an approach with a very generous cash offer. We actually had to stall him to prevent us encroaching upon your time of grief."

I felt Chris tap me thrice on my left shoulder. It was a childhood code we had developed for the many occasions when our parents were entertaining and we were tasked with being seen and not heard. This sequence meant 'let's see'.

"Mister Tyler, what is your client's offer?"

He gathered himself, as if he was about to reveal something momentous: "Two hundred and eighty thousand pounds sterling, to be paid in full and in cash, for the property and all items within, bar clothing."

The single tap on my right shoulder was agreement with my reaction: "Not accepted. The property itself is worth over six hundred thousand. The possessions inside, even after we have decided what to keep, will fetch several thousand on top of that."

Andrew's voice dropped: "But can you really expect that sort of return on a death house? Please, be reasonable."

'Death house'? I felt Chris's other hand hook itself through my belt to hold me back.

"I am being reasonable: you still have all your teeth."

He gathered himself visibly before replying: "Alright, then. I am authorised to go up to three hundred and twenty thousand."

I stared at him until his gaze fell: "If I open this door, you'll wake up in hospital. Post-traumatic stress is like that. I'll have no memory of accidentally maiming you."

Mister Tyler beat a hasty retreat. I closed the door to the accompaniment of Chris's applause.

There are two things I lost during my three tours in Iraq: the first is the obvious one - friends got killed. When it comes right down to it, the silly arse orders - obeyed like the world would end if they weren't - and the substandard kit were only symptoms of the fact that we shouldn't have been there. We were completely unprepared for what we encountered. A lot of good men died for a cause that was far removed from 'freedom'.

The second loss is the thing that affects me most. Despite my threat to Andrew Tyler, I came back without any of the grim, lingering residues so many are afflicted with. I just lost my faith in people. When you couldn't tell the difference between a herder and an insurgent, you had to be on your guard all the time. It stayed with me. Even on Evesham High Street, I watched for the movements and shapes that would betray an assault rifle under a long coat, a pistol concealed in a pocket, or a bomb in a backpack. I never got skittish, but constant wariness is tiring. When I told Chris, she burst out laughing, then apologised. It struck her that, when the other state of mind was tired boredom and resigned trudging from shop to shop, the tingle of hyperawareness, of being "sharp rather than blunt" would be her preference.

It is this remnant that brought our watchers to my attention. I was a squaddie, pure and simple. No specialisation or special forces for me. Luke Shaw went in straight from school, made Private, learned how to observe and what to watch for, but came out a Private. Which was

obviously not the career path the rather large group of gents and
ladies who started accompanying our movements had chosen. After a
little thought, I decided not to say anything.

We were sitting at the dining room table one night, working our
way through a dozen bottles of Hobgoblin – drunk was a state that
Chris and I had started to spend most of our evenings in. Without
warning, Chris pointed the top of her unopened fourth bottle at me
and asked: "Have you clocked the dark blue saloon that seems to be
wherever we are?"

I grinned. Silly of me to think she wouldn't notice: "Yeah. Plus the
overly casual civvies in new, dark, tailored clobber that seem to like
shopping in the same stores as us, and at the same time."

Chris' brow furrowed: "I've seen two or three couples like that.
Now you mention it, they did look a little out of place. You have any
ideas?"

I shook my head as I cracked open my fifth bottle: "Not really. I
guess they have a couple of near-identical cars, manned by two or
three teams of four on some kind of rota, just to try and keep us from
spotting them." I chuckled and raised my bottle in mock salute:
"Tag! We see you."

Chris giggled and we moved on to sillier things, and crazier reasons
for their presence, as the Hobgoblin supply dwindled.

Next morning, we both regretted moving on to the Black Tower
after the Hobgoblin ran out. The kitchen side revealed that we had
polished off three bottles. Thankfully, it had been Chris's turn to get
Dad up and settled, the both of us having tacitly decided that his
cleaning days were over. She muttered darkly, about my devious

ways, as I sauntered into the kitchen three hours after she had had to drag herself downstairs. By way of apology, I offered to buy her lunch in town. Dad, once settled, was immovable. Toilet breaks he managed on his own, providing nothing obstructed the direct route from chair to toilet and back. We made sure of that and then decamped for a leisurely lunch.

When we came back, three hours later, the front door was wide open and Dad was gone. Frantic enquiries of the neighbours gave no leads - most were at work and their houses empty except for pets, or children engrossed in online diversions. We called the police and then had to call the specialists who had tried to treat Dad, just to prove that we had not deliberately left him so he could wander off and remove a burden from our lives. Dad did not deviate from his routine for anything. For him to have gone, someone would have had to have taken him. Amidst the confusion and guilt, Chris took me to one side.

"Our watchers are absent."

She was right. So, after a quick discussion, we told the police about them. The result was that we started to get looks that Chris told me were just like the ones people gave Dad, before they stopped coming to visit. As the police left for the night, one of the inspectors gave me a card. It was for a London clinic that specialised in treating post-traumatic stress disorders.

A week passed and nothing happened. The platitudes from the police rang ever hollower. One night, we were deep into another mutual drunk when Chris confided that while she was mortified, it was more because she felt relieved over not having to care for Dad anymore, than over his disappearance.

Ten days later, we were restocking at the local supermarket when I noticed a vaguely familiar couple nearby. I said nothing until I saw the dark blue saloon with its pair of dark-attired occupants outside. Without warning, I was consumed by an utter certainty that Dad was dead. Chris shouted something as I exited our car at speed, pre-combat adrenaline deafening me, and headed for the saloon. I saw the occupant nearest me react with shock, then I swung his door open and dragged him bodily from the vehicle.

"What did you do with my father?" His face paled, and I knew I had one of the culprits.

"Chris! Get the number plate and call the police!"

As I shouted that, he twisted in my grasp and brought a knee up into my groin, with everything he had behind the move. The world changed colour several times as I keeled over, clutching my balls. I heard Chris scream something, but the pain had reduced my world to a dark tunnel - with the car park and all other considerations at the opposite end.

By the time the police arrived, I was leaning on the bonnet of our car, sipping a coffee; the dark saloon and its occupants having beaten a retreat while I was floored. Chris had only just stopped fussing when the police set her off again, by arresting me for assault. Apparently 'Mister Wilson' had taken exception to my unprovoked assault, and was also very angry that I had 'upset his wife and family'.

Down at the police station, I maintained a stoic insistence regarding 'Mister Wilson', his accomplices, and their motives. The only thing it got me was a cell for the night, where I was meant to "cool off" and "stop being so bloody paranoid".

The next morning, an unhappy-looking officer released me while his boss stood to one side with an expression of frustrated rage on his face. Chris was waiting in reception with someone who I had to do a triple-take to recognise.

"Samantha?"

The vision in a tailored business suit smiled enigmatically: "Later, Luke. Go with your sister while I finish off here."

Within an hour, Chris and I were sat at our dining room table, with Samantha and her partner Deirdre sitting opposite. The second round of coffees was cooling in front of us. I lifted a hand to still the chatter.

"I'm a bear of little brain today. Why don't you slowly and clearly explain how you arrived to extract me from custody?"

I paused and pointed at Chris: "No interruptions."

Samantha smiled as Deirdre giggled. Then she leant forward and placed a business card in front of me: "I'm a lawyer. Dree and I have a very well-thought-of practice in the heart of London. Our clientele values our discretion and, consequently, the very occasional request we make is given priority attention."

"So this has nothing to do with a grand conspiracy involving the goons and their masters." I shook my head, exaggeratedly, in mock disappointment.

Chris burst out laughing and punched me in the arm: "Stop being a tit, Luke. Sam and Dree haven't been home since they landed yesterday night, after a holiday in Switzerland. Sam got my message, and appeared on the doorstep earlier, saying it was already solved."

Samantha made a deprecating gesture, but Deirdre caught her hand, shaking her head in disagreement: "Sam was beside herself when she got your message. Wouldn't hear of easing off until you were freed. Quite a lesson in the arts of persuasion I've had over the last few hours."

I bowed my head: "Thank you. I apologise for letting my anger get the better of me."

Samantha leant forward: "Don't be silly. You and Chris rescued me from arsehole exes enough times."

We all grinned at that. Samantha had been a popular girl at college, but unfortunately possessed no talent at all for spotting a good man amidst a crowd of good-looking ones - or realising that she had far more than lesbian 'tendencies', for that matter.

Deirdre leaned on Samantha's shoulder: "Which brings us, tangentially, back to the topic of your strange followers. Don't you have any ex-service friends you could call? From what Chris has said, someone should be able to get a line on your fan club."

I froze. The idea simply had not occurred to me.

"Told ya." Deirdre grinned at Samantha, kissed her cheek, and picked up her bag.

Samantha stood and flicked her hair back: "It would be a good idea. Something about this situation - from how it happened to how easily it disappeared when I made a fuss - sits wrong with me."

With that, they said their goodbyes and left. Chris and I just sat until hunger pangs headed me toward the kitchen cabinets. As I am an awful cook, my clear intentions broke her daydream. I ended up peeling the spuds - as usual.

After dinner, I started calling round. It took a few hours, as squaddies will gossip like girls on a night out, much as they'll deny it. In the end, I had three numbers. One for Pete - an old friend - who had transferred out and was 'doing something fishy' in London, one for a mate who was with a PMC that had offices in Croydon, and one for the mate-of-a-mate whose girlfriend worked at GCHQ.

The GCHQ lead fizzled out quickly, as bloke and girl had parted ways over his indiscretions about her work. The PMC lead got me two offers of work: Somalia or Boston. The Somalian one paid more, but apart from that, he didn't have a clue. The London lead got me an 'unobtainable' tone.

I had barely replaced the receiver and stood up when my mobile phone rang, showing as an 'unknown number'. I shrugged in reply to Chris's querying look, then answered the call.

The gent who spoke was unfamiliar: "Mister Curlews is busy, but he knows you would not call unless it was a significant problem. Please describe the situation and he will contact you if he can help."

There was no percentage in being shy about it, so I told the whole story. The gent thanked me and then hung up.

"Is that normal?" Chris passed me a bottle of Hobgoblin, before settling into the armchair on the other side of the coffee table.

"Not even. I have no idea what I may have just set off."

We drank and chatted but nothing else happened. Comfortably numb from a decent, but not excessive, drunk, I hit the sack about midnight, leaving Chris asleep in the armchair with a blanket tucked around her.

I woke without drowsiness, fully alert and reaching for my rifle. The clock showed a little after three in the morning. I was about to write it off as a dream when a rapid series of 'pops' sounded outside. If my window hadn't been ajar, I wouldn't have heard a thing.

As I said: I have no specialised military training. But I had witnessed the violent ends of several special operations, usually ones that had gone badly pear-shaped. That popping noise was a suppressed automatic, one with a burst fire option. This made whatever was happening outside unusual, illegal - and irresistible.

Wriggling out of bed, I dragged tracksuit bottoms on before moving cautiously over to the window. A few minutes' observation gave me a pretty good idea of what was going on: our quiet residential street was hosting a terribly polite melee. I saw careful sniping and silent hand-to-hand, then watched, disbelieving, as all the combatants disappeared into cover when a car drove by, only to emerge fighting even more viciously. This went on for about fifteen minutes before it went quiet. Then a figure hopped over the front wall, straightened up and waved at me like this was a perfectly normal early morning.

The anonymous figure moved quickly to stand below my window, and looked about, before looking up and speaking quietly in a familiar voice.

"Got your call. No idea what those wankers are in to, but it's blacker than black. Which means a few can fall off the grid as easy as bricks down a well. Can't help any more, but I hope this evens the odds a little."

This was unbelievable: "Pete?"

He nodded and then turned to lope away through next door's Leylandii, waving a farewell just before he ducked into the foliage. Silence returned, except for the hiss of an electric car's tyres receding.

Next morning, there was no trace of the incident. Even when I looked hard, there was nothing. No spent brass, not even a cracked window or some chipped paint. I only told Chris because she insisted, after I tried to gloss over my reason for being so preoccupied. Then we both spent an hour making curtains twitch as we prowled the neighbourhood.

We returned home with a sense of moving through a dream. But as we entered the kitchen, our disassociated mood was lifting. I became aware of someone standing by the range just as the bullet slammed into me. I hit the floor moments before Chris, who fell across me. With an almost surreal gentility, my senses faded out and darkness fell.

Snow landing on my face woke me. I tipped my head to see what pinned me down, and saw Chris slumped across me. She was naked and her skin was grey-blue in the light of the fire.

Fire?

I struggled to sit up, but only managed to wedge my head up against the fence at the foot of the garden, and set off agony in my chest. We were lying in the vegetable plot, and I had not the slightest idea how we came to be there. Looking left, I saw a shovel stuck in a pile of earth. Between us and it was the opening of what had to be a shallow grave. Turning my head with difficulty, I saw that the firelight came from the conflagration that was consuming our home. As I gasped in denial, a distant voice came from my right.

"This domicile had to fall. It is the second time I have been called here. It will not happen again."

I twisted my head, ignoring the shooting pains in my neck. Closer than the voice indicated, but still a way off, a figure in yellow robes stood, its pale crown reflecting the flames. The face was in profile and, from what I could see, seemed to have sustained some brutal scarring at some time in the past.

"Why spare us?" I had no idea where the question came from, but as I spoke it, it seemed the right thing to ask.

The figure did not move. The lips did not move either. But a reply came: "I spared only she. Possessing eyes like hers, she could not be complicit. As for you; you were already here. I would venture that my arrival interrupted your interment."

My body chose that moment to spasm in pain and chill. By the time I had it under control, the figure had gone. I dragged Chris to lie along me and wrapped her as best I could. We lay there and shivered as morning arrived, along with the emergency services.

Both of us spent a month in hospital. On top of our mutual cases of mild hypothermia, Chris had been tasered, beaten, and carved like a piece of tooled leather. Even so, she only succumbed to shock and blood loss after escaping the house. My being shot once seemed trivial in comparison, for all that the bullet came within a half-inch of killing me.

While we healed, Samantha worked wonders on our behalf. After a short, whispered conversation with me about the fight I witnessed, I gave her Pete's number, and she patted my arm, saying that things would be fine.

The police pounced on the pair of us as soon as the doctors would let them. Right on their tails were a host of gutter press. The questioning got really nasty, with insinuations, and then outright accusations, of incest and sado-masochism. Apparently, we were a ten-day sensation in the tabloids and on the 'net. Then someone leaked the forensics results, confirming that there were eighteen bodies amidst the ashes of our home. Thankfully, the media circus went into overdrive elsewhere. The police, however, were still sure that we had been willingly involved. I gave as good as I got, but Chris was plainly not coping. So I called Samantha.

The next thing we knew, some polite and gentle paramedics whisked us away from the hospital, in the dead of night, by private ambulance. By morning we were ensconced in a luxurious recuperation facility. Samantha came in as the nurses finished fussing over our morning care routines. As breakfast was served, she dragged a chair over to sit between our beds.

"Eat while I talk. I don't mind. Oh, before I forget: Dree says 'hi'."

We slowly started to eat, and Samantha pulled out her laptop.

"Your stay here is 'compliments of' some people who know you both had nothing to do with what happened. When you leave, you have a new home just north of Lewes, in East Sussex, bought and paid for with the generous compensation you have received. That money comes from associates of those who died in your house: the deceased being the ones who paid 'Mister Wilson' and his colleagues. The settlement comes with a comprehensive non-disclosure agreement, but, as you know nothing, I didn't see that as a problem."

She was right, but I badly wanted to know. As it was, answering that need could wait a while. We signed, and became immune to poverty for a couple of decades.

Samantha sent the confirmation off, and had just put her laptop away when Chris pointed a fork at her, a stern look on her face.

"Sam, what aren't you telling us?"

Samantha actually looked about, before sliding her chair forward until her head was as close as she could get between both of ours.

"A whole lot of well-connected people backpedalling faster than I have ever seen. The bodies in your house have been identified as those of your assailants and ten others, eight of whom are very highly placed, either by political standing or wealth. The identities of the remaining two have been withheld from all record. Pete reckons that you two are almost guaranteed a free ride until the peers of those who died are dead and buried."

She paused and grinned at me: "Interesting chap, your friend Pete."

I shrugged: "Don't look at me. I only knew him before he became a covert actions superstar."

There was a brief smile, then her expression turned serious. She reached out to hold a hand from each of us: "What happened will never come to light. It was so secret that I doubt there are more than half a dozen people who have even the vaguest idea. Unfortunately, everyone I have consulted agrees that your father is dead. I'm so sorry."

After that, she left quickly. Chris and I cried a little, but, on top of everything else, it only added to the numbness we were both experiencing.

A month later, we moved into our new home. It was actually a very nice house on the outskirts of Lewes, with neighbours who were disinclined to pry, beyond introductions, and nods when we saw each other thereafter.

The second night after we moved in, Chris and I sat in armchairs either side of the blazing fire. We had a bottle of Black Tower each, and were about halfway in, when Chris started to speak in a scarily flat tone.

"I thought they'd killed you, I really did. There was so much blood and they were laughing when they pulled the taser needles out of me, before they carried me up to mum and dad's room. They had taken all the furniture out and pulled the carpet up. Did you know there was a floor safe hidden below the carpet under their bed? They'd ripped it open. The rest of the floor was covered in some complicated pattern, like a square that had been bent out of shape. There was all sorts of writing around it too. That was all I saw before they dumped me on the floor and cut all my clothes off. I thought they were going to take turns raping me, but the fattest one started carving patterns into my tits and tummy with a piece of black stone – it looked like one of those prehistoric knives we saw in the museum when we were kids.

When I started screaming, one of the others shoved my knickers into my mouth. After that, the fat one opened this tatty book and started tearing pages out, rubbing them in my blood and then passing them to the others. When he finished, they just tossed me into the corner by the door to the en suite. I saw they had placed pages at various places on the design. The fat one told the goons who had been following us to get out because the 'fetish bit' was over. Those that remained stripped naked and started chanting stuff; it sounded like they were all using different languages. My sight went blurry and then to only black and white. I thought I was about to bleed to death, but the colours came back when he appeared in the room. They were too intense, like the contrast was up to high, but I reckon it was something about his yellow robes, because the effect moved like his tatty cloak was giving off some weird effect that just made things seem sharper."

She paused to take a swig, and I hit my bottle hard. Yellow robes? Could he have been the same person as the scarred gent in the garden when I came round?

"Chris, did he have a crown on? Made of thin bands but with high points?"

She looked at me, the colour draining from her face: "You saw him too?"

"Only briefly. He said that he had spared you because of your eyes." As the words slipped out, I realised I should never have released them.

Chris's eyes widened and she waved her bottle at me: "He said that! Wait. Wait. Let me get there."

Her voice dropped back into the scary monotone: "He just walked slowly around the room, as the fat one at the centre of the pattern shouted things at him in a language that seemed to have no vowels. I got the feeling that he was deliberately ignoring the fat man. But when he replied, he spoke English."

"What did he say?"

Her brow furrowed and her lips moved as she ran through the words, presumably to make sure she got them right: "I have been here before. I warned that I would take another summons badly. Now still your tongue; your words have no purchase upon me."

"What next?"

"He didn't say anything else, just looked about at the naked people, and as he looked away from each of them, they dropped to the floor and started eating the pages. They had my blood smeared all over their faces and hands but they didn't stop. No. That's wrong. They *couldn't* stop."

She looked at me, an expression on her face from so long ago, back when she believed that her big brother could answer any question she asked: "How do I know that?"

I didn't know, despite a cold terror rising within. So I told the first lie that came to mind: "They muttered about it between mouthfuls."

Chris nodded, mollified. She continued speaking, using the tone I was starting to dread.

"When the last page had been eaten, they all collapsed. He walked round them, over to me. Looked down at me, looked me straight in the face. His eyes had specks of gold in their grey. He said 'your eyes are like hers'. Then he smiled -"

She screamed. Chris screamed, and I nearly fainted from the horror in it. Instead, I launched myself over to her and grabbed her in an embrace, clinging like she would disappear if I let go. The scream choked off and after a few sobs, I heard her whisper: "Not a mask."

She struggled frantically within my hug, so I let go. She pushed me away and blinked back tears before saying: "That's when I passed out."

With that, she fainted into my arms.

The next morning, Chris asked me just how drunk we had been, and if she had done anything stupid while off her head. I told her that she had just dozed off. As well as the traumatic memories I didn't want her to revisit, I was sure that something I said during the previous night's conversation was something she must not be reminded of. The wine had done a good job of messing up the finer points in my memory as well.

The drunken monologue seemed to clear something from Chris's psyche. Over the following few days, she came out of the withdrawn state she had been in since the fire. Within a week she had secured work with a small agency in town, telling me sternly that just because we had money, it was no reason to laze about. I was ordered to get a hobby.

So I joined an archery club and found an aptitude under the lifelong wish to try the sport out. By the following autumn, I had become one of the staff. From what we had come through, the outcome seemed generally good. Christmas was a lot of fun, with Samantha and Deirdre joining us for a week of drunken silliness broken only by bouts of overeating.

It was less than a week from the anniversary of the fire, when I received a call from the agency where Chris worked. She had collapsed and been rushed to hospital. I paused only long enough to get details of the hospital, before charging out of the club.

Chris looked pale against the pastel sheets, and her touch felt light. She smiled wanly at me. I asked the nurse for some privacy.

"Chris. What happened?"

Her stare caught and held my gaze: "A client remarked on the gold specks in my eyes. I remembered."

The room lurched in my vision as my heart rate doubled: "What did you remember?"

"I never got a chance to thank him for saving me."

I stared, because her client had been right. Since when did my sister have those gold specks in her eyes?

"He knew, Chris. He knows, even."

"But I knew him, Luke. From somewhere."

"Probably a dream." Again, I knew that I had said something utterly wrong, yet simultaneously absolutely right.

Her eyes widened, a flush crept up her cheeks, and she whispered: "You're right. From a dream."

I dropped my head and sighed hard. Looking up, I grinned: "So no more drop-down-dead at work moments?"

She smiled back, but her voice had traces of that monotone: "No more. Promise."

The hospital let her out the next day. I brought her home and fussed over her for a couple of days, then she threw me out, telling me to go and shoot some arrows at my fears.

The following night was the anniversary of the fire. I packed up early and came home so we could be together. We had a takeaway and laughed our way through a couple of appalling B-movies featuring improbable monsters in unlikely places, feasting on stupidly naïve people. We both drank quite a lot, but made it upstairs without incident. As I turned to enter my room, I felt her hand on my shoulder. I turned round to stare down at her, and the specks in her eyes seemed almost luminous as they caught the bedroom lights.

"I love you, big brother. Thanks for looking out for me."

She grabbed me and I crushed her in a hug so she couldn't see the tears start in my eyes: "Love you too, Chris. Sleep well."

I held her close until I felt a stirring in my underwear, then pushed her gently away; I'd had more to drink than I thought. We separated and, as I turned my back, I heard her door close.

The room swam as I closed the door, confirming I had drunk a lot more than I thought. I grinned and fell onto my bed. Undressing and showering could wait until I had sobered up a bit.

The cold woke me. I rolled over and saw the bedroom door was open. Struggling upright, I paused in a sitting position until the pounding headache receded. Heading out onto the landing, I saw that Chris's door was open as well. Sticking my head in, I saw that her bed was empty.

With a grin on my face, I headed downstairs to ridicule Chris as she struggled to relight the fire. In the lounge, I found only a flickering candle relieving the pre-dawn gloom. In its fitful light, I saw Chris's nightgown folded neatly on her armchair.

Panic filled me and I stampeded about the house, but Chris was nowhere to be seen, and nothing of hers had been taken. Outside, the snow had started again. A thought took me and I rushed out of the back door, to see small footprints leading across the garden, toward the field gate. I had to hurry. The snow was getting heavier. I sprinted out onto the Downs, following the footprints.

She lay under the sullen skies, her blue eyes staring at nothing and her only garment a yellow scarf twisted about her wrist. I dialled by touch, blinded by tears. I never expected the aftermath to drive her to this. Why hadn't she come to me? That's what we always used to do: take our hurts to each other for healing.

The emergency services were gentle, as were the police. I moved as directed and sat when told. I gave them every detail they asked for, without holding anything back. There was no point in reserve any more.

Samantha and Deirdre moved me into their place in the city, after I had been found wandering the streets, drunk and crying out her name, for the third time. When I'd settled in their spare room and managed a week sober, they sat me down one evening and gave me the yellow scarf.

It was made from the purest silk, they told me. So pure that it must have cost a fortune. The embroidery was done with incredibly fine gold thread. It seemed to be an abstract pattern. When it was unfolded, I recognised it. That's when I cried. Samantha and Deirdre left me to my grief, ignorant of the depths they had unwittingly opened.

The scarf had been my mother's. The purest yellow silk, embroidered in spun gold with an apparently random pattern - that actually had a single interpretation.

When Dad went insane, I desperately researched causes and treatments. After that revealed nothing, I turned my obsessive attentions toward researching the play, which also proved to be a fruitless quest. So I dived into the apocrypha that had accumulated about the play, a trove that was rich with self-appointed experts and supposedly-hidden knowledge. Amongst many baleful references to a 'pale king', I did find the occasional snippet that had some bearing on reality as we know it.

Like the fact that if you look deep into the constellation of Aries, you will find a few dim stars that are part of the Hyades Open Cluster. If you chart those stars, and then dial their positions back a few thousand years, the pattern formed matches the pattern on my mother's scarf.

Something in the pattern caught the attention of my drunken subconscious one night. It made me recognise the faint resemblance that I'm sure I would have missed had I been sober. It was only when I thought to use an interactive star map, which allowed me to scroll back the centuries, that I found the exact correlation. The star at the centre is called 20 Arietis. I have no idea what significance that has, except for a few notes that mention about 'somewhere beyond Arietis', and context locates it as the one in the Hyades.

What happened to Chris and I became clear, when you added the implications of the scarf. My father did not fall victim; he fell because he did something that every occult work I have ever read, no matter how extreme, has warned against even contemplating: he called up the pale king.

I heard the yellow-robed gent say: "I have been here before."

That would have been the night my Dad went 'away' – one hell of a warning. Mum just put the play back in the floor safe and re-laid the carpet, putting the bed on top as well. So far beyond good old middle-class English denial, it beggared belief.

"Your words have no purchase upon me." That's what he said. Ten people, with power and money to spare, spent a long time preparing and getting all the right gear. They may as well have being trying to command the wind. But he commanded them, and didn't even have to speak.

I had lost my parents. With what I'd discovered, that was no great trial. But their stupidity cost me my sister.

The worst thing was that when I passed a certain point in my drinking, I became sure she wasn't dead, despite the cold body I had cradled in my arms. Not dead in any way that mattered, at least. She had gone to join his court, 'somewhere beyond Arietis'. I hoped she had met that someone from her dreams, so she wouldn't be lonely.

Samantha and Deirdre tried their best, but I was a determined drunk of the worst sort: I craved the place where I believed Chris wasn't dead. As that place could only be found after drinking a bottle or two of spirits, quitting was not for me.

In the end, I left their spare room and moved into a bedsit over an off-licence in Bromley. The owner spoke English poorly, and was delighted to have a tenant who spoke passable Pashto. Over the following months, I managed to keep myself from being a hermit by forcing myself to work to subsidise my drinking. The fortune had been for both of us. I wouldn't waste it on me. I did whatever came up locally, so I didn't have to spend precious booze money on commuting.

Christmas came round, and I hit rock bottom. Drunken fantasies had hammered my feelings for my sister through lifelong denial. When I emerged from the three-day drunk that had caused, I knew something in me had broken. I spent New Year's Eve curled in a foetal ball, so drunk that I couldn't get the bottle to my lips. Naturally, when I sobered up enough, the bottle hit the mark, and down I went again.

As New Year's Day ended, I had shifted from floor to bed, and was only ruinously drunk. With a start, I pawed at my pocket. The scarf was gone! It had become so precious that it was like losing a limb. I tore the place apart, but the last thing that had touched Chris was gone. Slumping down in misery, I dragged myself into a corner and cried.

I must have slept. The room was gloomy but, in the murk, something moved. The scarf! I must have tied it onto the door handle at some point, then missed it in my drunken search. With that, I realised that I was the closest to sober I had been in a while. I also realised that the door was open. The knotted scarf seemed to be hanging unsupported in the darkness of the hall.

"The keeper of that frippery was her choice." The yellow-robed gent's voice came from far beyond the darkened hall. Its implications froze me to the spot.

Chris just faded in from nowhere. She stood naked in the doorway, the scarf twined round her wrist.

She held out her hand: "Come away?"

Blood hammered in my temples and I swallowed, mouth gone dust-dry. I looked at the desperate scrawls and clippings on the walls and ceiling, all interspersed with pictures of Chris. I saw the empty bottles heaped carelessly, the flies on the cartons stacked in the overflowing bin, the stains on my tracksuit.

I wasn't drunk. I was insane.

With that admission, things became clear. I stripped naked and washed away this world's dirt, my illusions, and any reality without her.

Then I took Chris's hand and we walked into the darkness, following the pale king.

THIRTEEN OF THE CLOCK

From whence they came, none could say. Guards and servants alike could not attest to seeing them arrive, or even recall having noted their striking attire as they passed by. Somehow, they navigated the labyrinthine corridors that led to the halls of the masquerade unguided, unseen - and thus unchallenged.

It is without contestation when they entered into that tumultuous, stately throng; both appeared just after the giant grandfather clock in the centremost hall struck seven.

Two figures of monochrome hue; one garbed wholly in bloody reds: gauchely appearing as a victim of the plague that raged without. The other displayed an incredible variety of yellow shades throughout his ragged finery: ranging from spring blossoms, through canary feathers, to tones of icteric decay.

He in red wore a mask to match his attire, spotted with sanguine ruin. The yellow guest sported a pallid creation of horrid countenance, thankfully occluded in the main by his long, backward-peaked hood.

They circulated in a leisurely way for hours, moving with ease from hall to hall amidst the revellers. In truth, their passing was as of pikes through minnows: not once did they have to cede their progress to other guests – the gathered host simply parted before them, then rejoined behind.

Many remember their passing, or experiencing their chill proximity, but none can recall having heard them engage another guest in conversation, or even utter a single word.

It was in the central hall when at last they came face to face, right under the ebon face of the towering clock. They regarded each other with postures that told much to those who witnessed it: he in red exhibited surprise, canting his head slightly as if somewhat taken aback. He in yellow merely tipped his head in polite acknowledgement: that of peers meeting upon a chance encounter.

When they leaned toward each other, as if preparing to exchange quiet words, many were the conversations stilled as the curious sought to eavesdrop.

What may have chanced from that fraught discussion was confounded by the striking of midnight upon the great clock. At the twelfth stroke, the red guest straightened up and pulled his mask away to reveal naught but a void behind.

A swirling hush fell as horrified breaths were taken. But then the clock struck for a thirteenth time, and he of the pallid mask spoke.

"Time - is of no consequence."

Then his features contorted into a smile repugnant beyond endurance, for, in truth, he wore no mask.

Ere the first step of the inevitable, terrified stampede fell, the bearer of the red mask had fled.

CRESSIDA'S WINDOW

A quiet Wednesday eve in the Merrie Harriers, and the slot machine and I had had a tiff. It wouldn't let me win any of my money back. So I was off sulking, in the farthest corner from the damn thing, when I noticed Henry Suells come in, a sizeable package under his arm and an expression of seeking on his face.

It seemed that my luck wasn't in at all. By the time I'd worked out he might be looking for me, I'd been spotted, and his face fair lit up as he headed for me like a terrier after a rabbit.

"Hello, Henry."

"A good evenin' to yer, Mister Matt. Yer just the gent I bin lookin' fer."

Feeling somewhat less than delighted turned to rank curiosity, as Henry promptly ordered two full Harriers ploughman's, with gammon, and then added: "A pint o'the usual fer meself, an' another of whatever Matt's drinkin'."

He placed the package down with care, then rubbed his hands together as the drinks arrived. Seating himself across from me, he sank half a pint without pause for breath.

Pointing the index finger of the hand gripping the glass at me, he opened negotiations: "Now, I know you've seen yer fair share of odds 'n' curios, Matt, what with yer business. That stuff you took care of for Missus Maybell, when George passed, was a champion job."

The man had died leaving his wife nearly penniless. She was going to throw out the vast collection of Victorian erotica George must have squandered a fortune on. I simply suggested that it might be worth some money. Even after my twelve percent, it still cleared six figures, and widow Maybell had relocated to her granddaughter's place in Marbella soon after.

"Henry. You've just bought me dinner and a drink. Please, get past the flattery and tell me what you think you've found." I pointed to the package.

He was delighted: "Sharp as ever, Matt. Right then. This thing came to me a few years back. One of me boys got it when we cleared the Dorset place."

I shrugged.

He nodded in realisation: "Ah yes, that would be before you arrived. Old man Dorset liked his collectables, and the family lived like they were local gentry, for all that he was the last o' the line and the old money was runnin' out. It all went down on Black Monday in eighty-seven. Seems his idea of investin' had bin like spread bettin' usin' the stock market. Lost the lot, he did. So he drinks a bottle of whiskey, kills his wife with a shotgun, and uses the other barrel to blow his brains into their swimming pool. Daughter came home a couple of days later because her university wanted paying and she couldn't get through to Daddy."

I glanced up from my ploughman's: "She found them?"

Henry nodded: "What was left. The dogs had chewed on Mrs Dorset, and Mr Dorset had been used like a bobbing apple by the crows. It was a right nasty mess."

I could understand that: "So, your lad found that?"

Henry looked about: "Not exactly. Said he'd bin in their library, luggin' boxes of books out, when he noticed one of the wood panels was crooked. So he went back later and had a look. Thought he was going to find a safe, he did."

Obviously not. I waved for Henry to continue.

"He goes over the whole room, lookin' for any other hidden bits, but there weren't anythin' else. This panel, he gives it a pull and off it comes. Said he didn't see it at first, because all that was behind the wood panel was another one. Then it started fallin' toward him, so he caught it. As he had the torch in his gob, it shone on the panel and he saw it was carved up something fine."

With that, Henry couldn't contain himself any longer. He pushed the condiments aside and lifted the foot-and-a-half-square box onto the cleared part of the table, with a grunt of effort. Opening it with a flourish - spoiled by having to stop the box from tipping over - he pointed at the contents: "What do you think?"

I reached out and lifted the browned newspaper. A square-cut corner-piece showed two finely carved nested squares around a central circle. That piece was nearly quarter of an inch above the border, which was an inch wide and displayed five straight ridges, carved with some skill, along their length. Lifting the paper away, I saw that the corner and border motif was common to all four sides.

At first I thought the piece was oak, blackened with age. Then I tried to lift it, and the weight made me realise that the whole thing had been carved from a single piece of ebony, probably Makassar, given the grain. At nearly a foot and a half per side, the wood itself was old, as I doubted that a tree of sufficient girth to provide the raw material for this panel had been felled within a century, at least.

Having established that the wood alone was worth a low four figures, it was time to establish the quality and subject of the art. I lifted the piece with difficulty, and the table creaked. Henry took one side of the panel, and we moved it back and forth until I could catch the relief work in a decent light.

The three stairs extending diagonally from the lower left corner caught my eye first. As I followed them, they cut back to reveal an edge, a walkway of some kind giving on to a broader way, as shown by the edge of that way, which ran to the right hand edge of the picture. Upon those steps, captured at the moment of stepping down onto the lower way, a figure in voluminous robes was the focus of the piece.

The folds of the cloth were deep, and, at side and rear, thick tassels revealed what may have been the ornate fringe of a formal cloak. Behind the figure, being carried in the off hand, was something long and thin. Possibly a rod, scabbard or similar; angled down and back, adorned with cords or threads that seemed to be twining in a breeze.

The figure had a pectoral over the robe, possibly the upper fastening point of the cloak. The face was obscured from nose to under the chin, although the contour suggested a filial over the nose, possibly from a mask or three-quarter helm under the cloth? Upon the head was a hood with a backward peak that looked pleated. About the head was the immediately recognisable circular representation of an aura of some kind. Arching to either side, tattered wings spread from the figure's back, with no hint of feathers or such. Bat wings or similar?

Beyond the figure, and extending away from the walkway, was an expanse of water, with hills of an almost pumice texture, coming down to the water's edge, on either side. Perspective showed that the expanse of water was broad. A lake or deep water port?

In the upper left corner, two towers showed beyond the hills: the left one plain with an onion dome roof, the right one a minaret with a 'double onion' dome roof. In the right upper corner, a single tower with an onion dome roof rose from behind a crenelated wall, quite possibly part of a sizeable keep. The skies between the towers and behind the figure were banded, as if by clouds against a sunset. All of the tooling was exquisite in its precision and detail.

All in all, a striking and atmospheric piece of unknown provenance. The figure was not an angel, of that I was sure. Nor demonic, either. Possibly the wings were like the aura, mutely describing supernatural attributes of the being portrayed. Questions aside, something about this work was fascinating.

I looked up at Henry: "I need to know more about this."

Henry looked uncomfortable: "That would be difficult, being that it's a bit nicked, an' all."

"Henry, no names need to be mentioned. As you said, I deal with curios all the time. Enquiries to establish provenance are always discreet. So where do I find Miss Dorset?"

He looked like I'd punched him: "Well, now. That would be difficult too."

"I said that no names would be mentioned."

Henry blushed: "She's married to me eldest."

"So she married the bloke who nicked it from her?"

He waved his hands in horror: "No, no. Me youngest found it, like. He's off in the States. Me eldest, he runs an import-export concern down in Newhaven."

"Henry, you're going to get me and Mrs Suells in the same room for a bit. I have a friend with a gallery in Newhaven."

"Calls herself Missus Anna Elizabeth Suells-Dorset. She and Larry got no kids either. Silly buggers are doin' what her daddy did all over again."

I pointed a finger at Henry: "Your boy own a shotgun?"

He paled: "You have a streak of bastard in you, Matt Crow. Did you know that?"

By way of mute apology, I bought the next round.

At the end of the evening, Henry said he'd call me, and that I could keep hold of the panel. It was gone midnight when I got the hefty thing indoors and under decent lighting. I revised my opinion: it was a masterpiece, even if I could not decide if it was haunting or merely disturbing.

Turning the piece over to see if the back had suffered any damage, I found it to be pristine except for a small scratch in the lower right hand corner. When I rubbed that with my finger, I realised it was deliberately incised, not a random mark. Bringing my valuation lamp in from the shop allowed me to use its magnifier to make out the marks. They formed initials: 'CL'.

I did what I could to find out more about the panel, but after a week of frustration, all I had was that the wood probably came from a tree felled in the mid-nineteenth century. It was time to seek help: a trip to London with the piece let me put it in front of Caspar, my font of all things woodworking-related.

He whistled as I slid the piece onto his table.

"Good lord, Matt. Where on earth did you find this?" He ran his hand along the edge: "Is this Makassar?"

I grinned and sipped my coffee: "A friend on behalf of a friend, and yes, I do believe it is. A single piece, too."

Caspar smiled wickedly at me: "How much to let this have an accident and turn up as some wildly expensive native carvings for my Kensington crowd?"

"No, Caspar. This piece has something about it. I want to know more, and you don't need the money."

He frowned momentarily: "All right then. Let's see what the art can tell us about the artist."

The next hour I spent admiring the work around Caspar's studio, wondering at the number of angelic carvings, while he brought various magnifying, illuminating and measuring devices to bear.

"Matt. I think I know who carved this."

I caught my cup before it finished its fall, and strode over to the table: "I'm sorry. I thought you said you knew who made it."

He grinned: "Well, don't get too excited. Except about the value. If I'm right, it's at least quadrupled."

Caspar ducked as I mock-swung at him: "From the top, you wood-charming fakir."

"Back in the mid eighteen-hundreds, six pieces, wooden carvings and reliefs of esoteric occult figures, done with incredible delicacy and detail, were sold by a Mister Sterlin Edwards, who had a studio in one of the nicer parts of London. They were notable because of the quality of the Makassar, and the fine instruments used. All six fetched staggering prices for the time, and enquiries were made regarding commissions and the like - that being the way for aspiring artists to make their fortune back then. The answer arrived in the form of a seventh piece, a shaman in shallow waters, surrounded by reeds. The work is said to have been so lifelike that it unnerved many who viewed it. After that was sold and safely out of Sterlin's hands - his premises having suffered two attempted burglaries, forcibly repulsed, while the piece was there - I guess you could say that enquiries turned to demands. Which is when Sterlin confessed he did not know the artist, just the man who brought the pieces to him to sell. The last detail is the one you'll like: the only signature mark on each piece was the initials 'CL' cut into the base."

I came back from picturing the scenes he described with a start: "Like this one!"

"Exactly. I am pretty sure that what you have here is the eighth piece: the piece that never made it to market. A lot of people expended a lot of effort to find it, and the artist. Sterlin stupidly let it be known that he had been told by the man that the artist was working on another piece."

"That was the end of him, I'd guess."

"Correct. Murdered by persons unknown in a most unpleasant manner - involving hot pincers, apparently."

"So we have a rich and unscrupulous bunch of collectors rabid for a new piece by this anonymous artist. There would have been fortunes to be made and reputations to be ruined. No wonder the artist did a runner. Two of my sources from a decade ago are still working out of Edinburgh, instead of New York, because of millionaire trouble."

Caspar chuckled: "I think I know one of them, but that secret is safe with me. Anyway, it seems that one of our rabid rich had brains as well as money. Hired a few people to investigate. They followed the wood."

Of course. A chunk of Makassar like that would attract attention and need haulage. I went and got us both coffees from the kitchen.

I put Caspar's mug in front of him: "Where did the wood lead?"

He grinned: "Herstmonceax."

"You're kidding."

"Not a bit. It was purchased by a Mister Leyke, of Herstmonceax, in East Sussex. Just down the road from where you live."

"The 'L' in 'CL', maybe?"

"Good guess. Unfortunately, his first name was 'Gustav', and apart from his name on a bill of lading, that is where the whole thing went cold. But now I have seen the workmanship first hand, I will be surprised if 'C' was not of slight build - quite possibly a woman."

I paid Caspar what he asked for his time without haggling, then headed back home to Cowbeech with the piece.

Three days later Henry called, and the day after that I was sitting in Dominic's place in Newhaven. The chime above the gallery door rang as an over-exercised and over-tanned woman cautiously stepped in, accompanied by a younger - and far fitter - version of Henry.

"Mister Crow?"

Dominic pointed my way. I rose to meet them.

"Da said you needed to speak to Anna?" His voice was worried. With Henry as your pop, it was par for the course, I guessed.

"Yes. It's about a piece that recently came my way and I'm trying to track down a bit of its history. I asked Henry about a family that used to live in the village and he sent me your way." I noticed that Anna had paled under her makeup. Without further ado, I lifted the cloth from the panel.

Her face turned a shade of ghastly grey-white and she whispered: "Cressida's window," before fainting clean away.

I looked at Larry, and he at me, both of us as mystified as each other. Only Dominic, rushing in to help, broke the tableau and turned our attentions toward Anna.

She came round just as we were debating whether to call an ambulance or not. Sitting up, her eyes fell on the panel and she blanched before waving a hand at it: "Cover it, please."

I did so, with an apology. Then I set down next to Larry and Dominic. We must have shared a tripartite look of intense curiosity because she burst out laughing.

"You should see your faces!"

Larry nudged my knee. He was the husband, so it was my job to ask the questions that would get him in trouble.

"What is it about that piece, Anna?"

She waited, until I thought she wasn't going to say anything. Then she started speaking quietly, almost reflectively: "Dad was obsessed with it. Said it held a clue to the rest of the Dorset family fortune. According to him - but remember he'd only tell this tale when he was drunk off his head - the artist who did that knew about great-grandpa Dorset's big secret: smuggled treasures from Egypt, or the Amazon, or the Orient. The place changed with every telling. The main bit is that the artist promised to keep quiet, but great-gramps didn't trust him until he got some kind of hold over the artist. It was something serious, because the artist only worked for great-gramps from then on. The story goes that the artist's only chance of revenge was to carve clues into his work, in the hope of someone figuring them out and stealing the Dorset's hidden treasures.

Dad said he'd seen the artist's other works, and they only had hints. This one had to be the one with the key. I lost count of the number of times I saw dad sitting in the study, staring at that panel, running his finger along the bottom of it, and swigging whiskey. Drove mum mad, and scared her too. She said dad could be a bit odder than his usual level of weird, after a night staring."

A hidden treasure? That was a step too far, I thought. Catching Dominic's eye, he pulled a face that indicated a similar level of scepticism. Larry just stared at Anna.

"So your dad had this panel on display?"

She shook her head: "He kept it in a cubbyhole behind a panel in the wall of the library. Said it had always been there."

Why would he keep it hidden? This didn't make sense at all.

"What about the woman you mentioned: Cressida?"

Anna looked at me, a puzzled look on her face: "That's what the picture is called: 'Cressida's Window'."

I had a lot of pieces and none of them fit together properly because the pieces that linked them together were missing. Or some were from another puzzle and only looked like they fit into this one.

"Who owns your parents' house now?"

Larry sat up and looked at me: "Funny you should ask, but we've just bought it. Her parents may have died there, but Anna says the happy memories and lovely grounds overcome that. Her folks would be happy to see her back in the old place."

There was nothing more to be found here. I thanked everyone and noted Dominic's request to be told the full story, then headed for Caspar's. I needed extra antique and curio investigating experience. If he couldn't help, he'd know who I needed to ask.

Caspar answered the door in a tatty grey tracksuit that was completely at odds with his daytime attire.

"Matt, it's eleven at night. What in the blue blazes are you doing?"

"Long story, Caspar. Feed me coffee and hear me out. I promise you'll either join me, or I'll get a room at a hotel, and send you a postcard when it's over."

He let me in, and I reeled off the encounter with Anna.

Caspar nodded his way through it, like he was imitating a cheap ornament from a vintage car. As I finished, he tipped his cup back, drank the lot, and then held it out to me: "Fetch. And don't come back without snacks as well. I need a few minutes alone to cogitate."

I vanished into the kitchen and threw together cold cuts plus every variety of cheese he had in the fridge. Adding pickle and two cups of fresh coffee, I headed back to find Caspar poring over a huge ledger that appeared to be some sort of gigantic scrapbook.

"What the hell is that?"

"Victorian public notices and newspaper clippings. You'd be surprised how many times I've found a snippet that leads to something useful. Your Miz Anna mentioned a word or phrase that rang a bell. Somewhere in here is the cause, seen in passing while I looked for other stuff. So I'll hunt, and you talk your way through our combined findings so far."

I sat down, wrapped cheese and pickle in a slice of beef, and multitasked - the polite term for talking with your mouth full.

"We have a panel of Makassar ebony of unusual size. On it is a relief carving of an unidentified chap in an unknown setting. The initials on the back lead us to believe that it is the 'lost' eighth work by 'CL', possible surname Leyke. He or she was a Victorian artist who disappeared, possibly due to patron trouble. Today I found that the piece is supposedly called 'Cressida's Window', and had been in the possession of the Dorset family for a long time. Apparently, it was thought - by some members of the Dorset family - to conceal a clue to something valuable. The piece is probably responsible for at least two murders."

Caspar looked up: "Two?"

"The dealer, and the man who brought the pieces to the dealer. After they tortured the dealer to death, he would have been the only lead."

He nodded agreement and returned to scanning pages: "Go on."

I looked at him: "On? That's it, isn't it?"

Caspar sighed and looked at me in despair: "Now make some inferences from the family legend back to what we know."

Inferences? What the hell? I shook my head and Caspar laughed.

After retrieving a lot of food, he settled back and waved at me in exaggerated disgust: "Some Sherlock you'd make! Anyway, the bits I picked up on are: Cressida would fit our 'C' initial. Great grandpa Dorset, or more likely his dad, could have been one of the patrons. The 'got some hold over' bit leads me to make a stretch – what if the middle-man blabbed, probably under torture, and prospective patron Dorset nabbed the artist for his own exclusive use? What if this panel contains Miss Leyke's SOS? That would be why it never came to market: because old man Dorset daren't let it out in case it gave his dastardly deed away."

He finished with a look of Hollywood-Machiavellian evil upon his face, and I burst out laughing.

"Good god. With an imagination like that, you should write film scripts, not chisel wooden angels."

"They are Seraphim and are highly regarded by a circle of affluent buyers. Collectable, they've been called. After paying ten thousand apiece, they can call them what they like." He grinned.

"What now?"

Caspar gestured to the tome that was doubling as his tray: "You keep me in coffee and shout at me when I drowse. Let's find what it was that caught my attention, then decide."

Three hours later, he shouted: "Got it! 'Cressida' was the word."

I leaned over his shoulder, and he pointed at a small piece of yellowed paper.

"What was that?"

"Probably a fragment from a parish notice or similar."

The words were faded, but by angling my head I could just about make them out:

Reward of 100s.

Offered for news of Miss Cressida Leyke.

Respond to Mr G. Leyke,

The Herons, Gardner Street, Herstmonceax.

Caspar looked up at me: "Seems our lady went missing and her father was serious about finding her."

I did some mental arithmetic: "That would be about five hundred quid nowadays. You were right. Miss Leyke didn't just stop carving; she vanished completely."

"And I know what we need to do next."

"You do?"

"Yes: sleep. Our mystery is over a hundred years cold. A few hours downtime and a decent breakfast won't hurt."

He had a point.

The next morning we belted through breakfast and headed for Cowbeech. I called Henry and got him to get Larry to open up the Dorset place. For all the previous day's discoveries, we were dealing with crimes and drama at least twelve decades past. What with the known crimes being unsolved and the others being only conjecture, we were more than a little stumped if we couldn't find something tucked away in that old house.

Caspar drove, and I spent the passenger time wringing information from Henry. The Dorset house had sold in '89, was left empty for about five years when planning permission could not be obtained, then changed hands again. From '95 to the end of the century it had been involved in a legal challenge over some of the covenants, which, in the end, were ruled to be binding upon any purchaser. Whatever they were - and Harry was on the landline to Larry about them - they had removed any interest in the place. When the ombudsman sold the place off, to recoup something from the bankruptcy of the previous owner, Larry snapped it up. The paper trail was a nightmare that had taken nearly a year to sort out, which was why he and Anna still hadn't moved in.

Harry came back on: "Larry says the covenants are simple: the bricks and mortar can't be changed at all. Ever. The grounds within fifty yards of the house must be kept as gardens; the plantin's are not covered, except for the beech trees to the north. Larry's sure that's it, because he's goin' to have to get the pool filled in and wanted to be sure there were no more nasty surprises."

We arrived in the late afternoon of a glorious early autumn day. Larry and Anna were there, along with Paul Dempsey: a top-notch builder, expert on historic building restoration, and an old friend of both Henry and I.

After swapping the usual catch-up commentaries, we settled to reviewing the house. Larry said that, apart from a few viewings by prospective buyers, the place was pretty well as it had been left when the removers cleared out and locked up. Paul said he'd looked the exterior over and it seemed in pretty good condition for a building which had been neglected for nearly two decades.

Larry looked at Anna, who nodded. He unlocked the French windows and opened them both wide. A smell of damp, and that odd odour of vacancy that pervades abandoned dwellings, wafted out. We gave the place a few minutes to air, while Larry and Paul chatted about filling in the pool. They had just got round to discussing motorised lawn-effect covers, when Anna slapped Larry gently: "We're not here to design the rebuild, love."

Larry laughed sheepishly: "Sorry. Got carried away."

We all traipsed in, to a slice of eighties luxury décor which had been tasteless even before time and damp got to it. The floors were bare, and wallpaper hung in great curls off the walls. We walked round the place, while Paul looked it over, then investigated the snooker room in the attic space. The snooker table stood festooned with immense, multi-tiered cobwebs. Anna took one look at the size of some of the inhabitants and announced loudly that if the secrets we sought lay beyond them, we were on our own.

Downstairs, Paul started pacing off lengths on floors and looking at the walls curiously.

"Larry, you haven't missed any doors, have you?"

Larry shook his head and Anna butted in: "This is every room I remember. Why?"

Paul pointed toward the centre of the house: "There's a void there, toward the far end from where we're standing. It should line up with the narrow fanlight I saw outside on the eastern end."

Caspar looked at me and grinned. A find!

Everybody got involved, under Paul's direction, and soon we had confirmed that the house was missing a chunk, no more than ten feet square, on the ground floor. The next trick was finding it. Peering in through the fanlight got us nowhere, as it had been painted over on the inside. Paul reckoned that the fanlight originally sat on top of another window, which had been covered and then blended in to match the finish of the exterior walls.

Henry beckoned to me, and we moved away from the group.

"Matt, Anna's dad had that panel hidden away in a cubby in the library. Unless me wits are addled, one side of the missin' space runs along the same wall of the library."

I patted him on the back and headed inside. Paul ran his eye over the wall in question and stepped forward to rap his knuckles along the wall visible between the shelves.

Finally, he stood back and turned to Larry: "There's a doorway there. I would guess that it's 'Victorian small' in size, and, after being boarded up, someone papered over it and put up the shelves that have been there ever since. I can get to it, but you're going to lose those shelves. Someone put them there to stay."

An ominous feeling stole over me. Why had the room been concealed?

Larry thought for a bit, then he and Anna went for a walk and a talk. When they came back, Anna was pale and holding Larry's hand tightly.

"Larry and I are worried what's back there. It's been hidden for a long time and no matter what my dad said, I don't think that it's treasure. Paul, lets find out."

Paul went out to his truck and came back with a sledgehammer, a yard-long crowbar and a toolbox.

"Stand back."

We did. He carefully tried various points on the heavy shelves with the crowbar, then shook his head and lowered the safety goggles he had on his forehead.

"Everybody out. This is going to be noisy and dusty."

The noise was loud; uncannily loud. There were sounds almost like screaming between the impacts and tearing. A half-hour later, he called us back in. He'd swept the debris back, and explained that the screaming sounds had been the eight-inch nails that had been used to anchor the shelves.

"Ship nails, at a guess. Way too substantial for this, especially as they were in places where they wouldn't help load-bearing."

Caspar ventured quietly: "But good places to make the shelves too much aggravation to move."

Paul nodded.

Where the shelves had stood was now a bare wall with patches of wallpaper, and the outlines of what had been the trim of a door frame. The boards had been pried away to reveal a plain oak door, the handle removed, and all holes sealed with some age-pitted and cracked filler. At the leading edge of the door, the heads of a pair of nails at top, middle and bottom could be seen.

Paul looked at Larry, who looked at me. Decision time. Whatever was behind there had been intended to remain hidden for posterity. I suspected that the covenants regarding the fabric of the house had been intended to abet that concealment. I nodded to Paul. He ignored the nails, instead chiselling space above and below the hinges, then driving the pins out.

He placed the crowbar and looked at me. I looked at Anna. She nodded and moved to stand behind Larry.

I waited a moment, to see if any better ideas occurred to me. They didn't. I gestured toward the door and nodded to Paul: "Time for the lost to be found."

He looked at me quizzically, then hauled on the crowbar. For a moment, nothing seemed to give. Then, with a crash and a 'whumpf' of stale air, the door grudgingly gave a little. With Larry, myself and Caspar gripping the trailing edge and pulling, while Paul applied the crowbar to lift the door when it caught on the floor, we got it back to right angles.

Anna shone Paul's torch in. Her eyes widened and her scream tailed off into a dead faint. Larry made a heroic dive and wound up sprawled on the floor underneath her. Paul picked up the torch, training its beam on a bed opposite the door. In the bed, a skull grinned at us from the raised pillows. A pocked robe, embroidered with peacocks and parrots, was wrapped about the skeleton. Little bones from bare feet were scattered on the floor, where they had fallen through the rails at the end of the bed.

Caspar cautioned us: "Touch nothing. It'll probably crumble if you do."

We peered through the doorway, not daring to venture in. Paul had been right. The fanlight did sit above a larger window, all painted out from this side. By what had been that window, a workbench stood, with tools scattered on it. I looked at Caspar and he nodded sadly.

There was so much unanswered, despite the grim truths in the room. But we daren't enter. Caspar's warning had been valid. It would need specialists to retrieve the body and examine the room.

I straightened up: "Larry, call the police."

It was a sombre group that met a week later. Over the intervening time, the police had talked to all of us, and we had spent a couple of days avoiding a few desperate-for-sensation reporters. With the body removed and the room pronounced safe, we had returned to examine the effects of what had been tentatively identified as the very late Miss Cressida Leyke. She had apparently died peacefully, sat on her bed. No signs of gross trauma or distress had been found. Any soft-tissue reasons would, of course, remain unrevealed, but in my mind's eye, she had seemed to be at peace.

The room had a primitive toilet, complete with bucket of sand and trowel, in one corner to the right of the workbench. Under the workbench were pieces of Makassar ebony. The tools had obviously been made for Cressida's small hands. Caspar cried unashamedly as he packed them back into the waxed canvas roll.

It was Anna who found the writings. Tucked into the gaps between headboard panels and frame were three slim pieces of wood, which

Larry spotted had been cut from the left-hand end of the workbench – the end least likely to be noticed by her captor. On each piece were tiny, carved letters. I made a trip to my shop to get the valuation light and its magnifier.

With lens to hand, and with additional light provided by Larry's torch, the four of us stood around the room and passed the last words of a woman a hundred years dead between us. None of us could bring ourselves to read them out loud.

10 February 1868 - Five weeks since Dorset's lackeys took me. He is a madman, raving about my works leading him to 'a place beyond the stars' where he will become a god. My work may be inspired by dreams, but nothing like what he contends. I have resolved to create as demanded, so that I may eat regularly.

7 May 1868 - Working in the drowsy state I find my best efforts within, I have created a window upon that place. In it, a nobleman has appeared. In dreams we have spoken, he and I. He says that when every detail has been wrought with tears and tools, this window will become my door.

18 Jan 1869 - It is done. Tonight I escape this place. Please tell my father that I did not suffer, and departed of my own free will. Andrew Dorset, I wish perdition upon thee.

We looked at each other and then at the panel: Cressida's Window. What an unspoken ordeal that poor woman must have suffered, to take her own life like that, thinking it an escape.

Caspar whispered: "What becomes of all this?"

Anna looked about: "We'll make it into a meditation room, with the window opened up and a little memorial altar under it. Caspar, you can have the tools. Matt, make us an offer for the panel."

She had suddenly transformed into the brassy siren I had originally suspected her to be, so I offered a price that made Caspar's eyes widen. Anna accepted it without hesitation, and I wrote a cheque on the spot.

As we drove away, Caspar stared at me in awe: "How did you have the balls to offer that little?"

"You see how quickly she returned to type? Cressida put her life into that panel. I bought it for myself, and I paid Anna a price in fair measure to her compassion."

Cressida's Window is mounted on my bedroom wall. Every time I spend a while looking at it, another detail becomes clear. I've started to add colours to it in my mind's eye. So much so that I dreamed of the place last night.

OPERATION SIGN

The statement of Andrzej Deszcz, as told to his daughter Rahel
(acting as his translator) in the presence of personnel from FIA(T),
officers of EPES 2 T-Force and representatives of BIOS on 26th
August 1945. Exact location withheld; southern England.

I was born and raised in Konary, a small village high in the Holy
Cross Mountains, east of Kielce city. There was nothing unusual
about the place except for the ruins of a castle on the opposite side of
the valley. It was so old it didn't even have a name. We just called it
'the castle' – everyone knew what was meant.

After the Germans, and then the Russians, invaded, not much
changed for us, except that the trader who brought luxuries from the
lowlands stopped visiting. The young men of the village had talked
of forming a resistance group, but, with only eight of them, it never
really got started. In the end, three of them headed down to Kielce to
seek the resistance. We never saw them again.

We all heard about the mass murders by members of the German People's Union, and lived in fear, until the news reached us that they had been disbanded because of those atrocities.

A few weeks later, Jacek came back from guarding his father's flock and said he'd seen lights in the castle. We asked him if he'd taken a bottle of vodka to keep himself company. He swore that he hadn't. We didn't believe him and carried on as usual.

Days later, Jacek didn't return from guarding the flock for the night. When a few of us went looking, we found Jacek face down by the lookout rock of his father's pasture. He'd been shot twice: once in the back, and once in the head. Six ewes were missing. We went back to the village, got together a hunt, and set off down into the valley, because that was where all the troublemakers and poachers came from.

It was early afternoon when we heard shots from back toward the village. We were so far down into the valley that it took us until early evening to get back. The fastest of us went ahead, and the rest of us heard more shots. When we arrived, there were bodies everywhere. Strange men and women in uniforms stood about in twos and threes as we were herded into the market square.

There was a man in a dark green uniform waiting. He called himself *Scharführer* Etienne Lutz, and his people were the last of the *Selbstschutz*. We knew that name: it was the one that the German-Polish fifth columnists used. They were bad people.

Then another man came out of the inn and he was introduced as *Oberführer* Reiniger. Using Lutz to translate, he told us that his SS-

Sonderkommando had taken over the castle, and we would be allowed to assist them in making *Unternehmen Zeichen* a success.

They told us to go about our business and that they would send a delegation to our headman when they wanted anything. After that, they went away, and left us to bury the eleven people they had killed. That told us how they really regarded us. Much vodka was drunk that night, but no solutions arrived. So next day we just carried on. There was nothing else we could do.

The *Oberführer* was good to his word, only bothering us when he wanted dairy products or fresh meat. The *Selbstschutz* may have been 'locals', but they were terrible hunters: they made too much noise for any game to ignore.

Lutz was a problem. He was half-German, half-Polish, and hated his non-Aryan side. Never a week went by that he and his four cronies didn't make things difficult for us. He would have gone further, but Reiniger's men arrived after a month. Eighteen proper *Waffen*-SS, and as their commander had said the villagers were not to be bothered, they made sure of it. The first night they were in town they took Lutz's man, who had been molesting Jacek's sister, and threw him into the ravine behind the village. He cried out for hours, but they didn't let anyone go and help him. In the end, the wolves from the hills above the ravine finished him off.

Don't make the mistake that some of the villagers did. The *Waffen*-SS didn't like us. They just hated the *Selbstschutz* more.

After that, things were quiet for a while. We kept a watch on the castle and recorded movements and times. It made us feel a bit better, knowing we had spied on the Germans, knowing we could prove it when the resistance arrived. The castle had a lot of men and women there. They had big generators, and tankers of fuel arrived at the end of each month. Over the first year, truckloads of material arrived. After that, it was just those stationed at the castle.

We almost got used to them. Lutz's men and women didn't come into town after the first three months, and the *Waffen*-SS were infrequent visitors.

During the summer of 1941, we started to see some of the *Allgemeine*-SS staff. They would come into town for Sunday lunch at the inn. On the whole, we had to reluctantly admit that they seemed like nice people. My younger daughter, Ewa, even got friendly with one of the young men, an *Oberschütz* Kurt Schaefer. I did not like it, but he seemed genuine enough.

That is how things progressed until late 1943, when Kurt warned Ewa that things were about to change at the castle. He seemed nervous. Before the end of that week, two trucks and a half-track arrived at the castle. At dawn the next day, we heard a lot of rifle fire. When Kurt arrived the following Sunday, he said that Reiniger and his personal staff had been executed under orders from the new head of the *Sonderkommando*: *Grüppenfuhrer* Diederich. He had told everyone that the operation had not been doing what it should, and that Reiniger had been using it for his own purposes.

In the middle of the following week, we were woken before dawn by the noise of the generators. When we peered out, the air above the castle had what looked like yellow and grey banners waving in it.

The following day, a dozen of the *Waffen*-SS accompanied several of the *Allgemeine*-SS to the inn. They all drank a lot, and quickly, in the way that people who wish to obliterate bad memories do. With hardly a word spoken, even between themselves, they left within the hour.

From then on, our nights would be torn by the howl of the generators. The noise heightened in pitch, to the point where it set off the wolf pack in the heights behind the village. To stand on one of the lookout rocks, seeing the colours flicker in the air above the castle, while generator noise competed with wolf song was eerie. Our priest left within a month, refusing any attempts to dissuade him. He said that something evil was happening in the castle and we, like him, should flee before it claimed our souls.

The wolves came closer than anyone remembered, even in tales handed down from earlier generations. Attempts to shoot them failed, as did attempts to drive or lure them away. As winter drew in, Konary became like a place lost in time. Villagers turned to older ways, after the departure of the priest. Offerings to spirits started to appear. The few devout churchgoers responded with evenings of chanted litany. The only place to get any peace was at the inn, where, no matter what, stony-faced villagers sat next to grim-faced SS, and both drank like salvation lay at the bottom of the next glass.

Between Christmas and New Year, the boy Radoslav said he saw an angel with golden wings drifting up the valley, level with the castle.

We all thought it was an eagle owl he saw, bathed in the odd lights above the castle.

On New Years day, no-one came to the inn from the castle. Two days passed, and we were about to go across to see, when Kurt came into the tavern and broke down in Ewa's arms. We gave him a lot of vodka and in his drunken misery, he told us everything he knew.

The castle had catacombs like all castles do, but this one had a huge basement alongside the rooms you would expect. The floor of that basement was made of polished black stone covered in strange symbols 'like twisted squares'. The engineering team had built electrical towers around the basement, with strange lights set up to shine into the centre of the room. While they were excavating to make a way to get the bigger equipment in, an ancient treasury had been found. That was the reason Reiniger had been shot: looting. He had been trying to hide the treasury from his superiors.

Diederich had explored that vault and found some things that were moved into the basement. They included a huge book, with covers made of black stone, and pages made of thin gold. After that had been placed on a table in the basement, only Diederich and his two aides were permitted to enter.

The troops that came with Diederich had no more idea about what the operation was trying to achieve than the SS who came with Reiniger. But sleeping at the castle had become a chancy thing. Dreams and nightmares, voices from the past, ghosts of dead relatives – all descended upon a sleeper. Kurt had taken to sleeping in a cave, halfway up the cliff behind the castle, after the number of suicides and unexplained disappearances reached double figures.

When we asked him about the disappearances, he just looked at us, with eyes haunted as no man's should ever be.

"We see them go to their beds, but when we go to get them, they are gone. Their possessions are undisturbed, their beds tidy. Nothing but little flakes of gold on the blankets."

At that revelation, the older villagers glanced nervously at each other. There was a folk tale about 'wolf's gold'. It had been told since the Dark Ages, and warned of 'golden snowflakes' being seen. The tale went that the finding of wolf's gold foretold of something dire, and the second sign was that any wolves in the area departed. As the wolf pack behind the village had been resident for as long as any could remember, we all agreed that their departure was unlikely.

Kurt descended further into a wretched state, so I let Ewa put him in her bed and watch over him. She said that he curled into a ball when the generators shrieked. At the inn, conversations died when we noticed that the wolves were no longer howling in reply.

For the remainder of that night I suffered evil dreams of monsters and impossibilities. The next morning, Kurt had already left, leaving his thanks to me with Ewa: a Luger pistol. He had made her repeat his words so I would get them exactly as he said.

"We are told that the operation is nearing completion. I believe that it is not a good thing. This may help, afterwards."

From that night onwards into spring 1944, I started keeping watch when I could. In the end, I took my post on the lookout rock that Jacek had died by. Just me and a little vodka against the chill.

The night he came was marked by the generators getting louder than ever before, and reaching a higher pitch than ever before. From the north, I heard far-distant wolf howls. They were not hunting howls; they were ones of warning.

The curtains of light above the castle ran through more colours than I could name, then, with a sound like thunder followed by a dying whine, the night was still. In the air between me and the castle there hung a figure in a hooded yellow robe, held aloft by great wings of the same colour. He turned a pale face toward me, and his gaze may as well have turned me to stone. If you ask me to be honest, I will tell you that I think he froze me there because he wanted a witness.

He flew slowly to the castle and descended into the courtyard. There were shouts and gunfire. After a few minutes, it fell quiet again. Then I saw movement on the crumbling battlements, as men and women climbed up to hurl themselves into space. They only screamed after they had fallen nearly all the way to the foot of the escarpment, and thus the noise was brief, but the silence, terrible. I still dream of that silence. Not the falling bodies, not the screams or the sound they made smashing into the cold ground. Just the silence as they fell is what haunts me.

The silence persisted until he lofted into the air from the courtyard. He flew up, then swooped toward the cliff behind the castle. I heard the man who, I admit for the first time today, could have become my son-in-law, die. I heard him scream my daughter's name with his last breath, so loud that it echoed. Then I heard her wordless scream echo in reply.

At that, the winged figure started across the valley toward my home. I ran like I have never run, before or since, to reach my home ahead of him. I made it by moments, and in my yard I stood with my arms spread wide in supplication, staring up at that golden angel of death.

"Spare her, majesty. She is my daughter, guilty only of love."

He looked at me and I saw golden lights spinning in the pits of his eyes.

"So very true." His voice was so calm, so cold; yet not indifferent.

Then he looked at a window above and, when I followed his gaze, I saw Ewa's pale face behind the pane.

"When the loss becomes too much, you can come to me."

I saw Ewa nod and cold clenched in my gut. But then he lifted into the sky, drifted out over the valley to about where I had first seen him, and then was gone as if he'd never been there. I looked about as something sparkled in the moonlight. A scattering of golden flakes drifted lazily down to settle in my yard.

I rushed to Ewa, and she cried herself to sleep in my arms. The next day, we heard wolves in the mountains behind the castle. Ewa was frantic, but I held her back. My thought was to let nature take its course and hopefully cleanse that place in the doing.

The other villagers said nothing, and I did not tell my tale, except to say that I was sure that the Germans had met with ill fortune. If anyone else had seen that night's events, they said nothing.

As winter released its grip, the castle disgorged SS-uniformed things that had once been human. They were too fast to hunt and too savage to corner, so we staked out blooded sheep. For three nights we killed snarling monsters that resembled nothing more than decaying corpses.

The wolves dealt with those we didn't lure to their deaths. For weeks afterward, we came across wolf-slain cadavers in ragged SS uniforms. None of them showed any signs of being eaten, either by the wolves that killed them, or any scavenger.

The war seemed to have forgotten us and the *Sonderkommando* at the castle. Spring turned to summer, and thence to autumn. It was as the last of the leaves fell that I awoke one morning to find my beloved Ewa gone, and wolf's gold in her bed. I had thought her recovered, but the yellow one had known better. The newly returned priest insisted that she had been ensorcelled.

But like I know he had wanted a witness that night, I know that he only took her because she had called him, or gone to find him. Another thing told for the first time here: I know that his taking her was a mercy. I know these things, I hate the knowing, and I loathe not knowing why they are true.

This is what happened. I swear it upon my beloved wife's grave and in memory of dear Ewa. Now will you grant us leave to dwell in your country like your officer woman said that you would?

Andrzej and Rahel Deszcz are recorded as having returned to Poland in March 1946. Their fate remains unknown.

Konary village was abandoned during the severe winter of 1951; the few remaining inhabitants moved to Kielce.

The ruins of Konary Castle now surround a hostel for hikers and trekking tours.

Barring this document, no Axis or Allied records of Operation Sign (Unternehmen Zeichen) have ever been found.

Curtain Call

Another dawn breaks about me with scant regard for the sensitivity of my eyes. I am in a park today, and seem to have the majority of my clothes. A quick pawing of my pockets reveals my wallet survived the night, for once, and I even find a matchbook, and a crushed packet containing a trio of cigarettes. The name on the matchbook is unfamiliar, and the cigarettes are a foreign brand. Russian, if I have to guess.

I squint about. The park is large and wooded around the edges. I haven't been here before, so I'll flee the light and head away from the dawn, across the longer expanse of grass, past the children's playground.

The stains on my hands as I lift the matchbook give me pause, then I strike up, and put the fold of card away, before considering the exact nature of what marks me. Holding my hands up, I see that my torn cuffs are stained dark red as well. That settles it: dried blood. I twist and turn to check the rest of me. The ruined shirt is spotted with it, and my left knee is near-solid. What crusts my bare feet is beyond identification, but I guess that there's blood involved.

Now to the next question: whose blood is this?

A quick peering about under my clothes, made all the easier given their state of disrepair, reveals that I am as hale and hearty as a dissolute undergraduate gets. Simple deduction leads swiftly to the conclusion that I am smirched with the essential fluid of others.

"Good morning." The lady with the Alsatian smiles and nods slightly as she speaks.

I wave a hand in acknowledgement, and smile in return.

Only the elderly are capable of blithely continuing with polite formalities in the face of aberrant peculiarity. They are a dying breed; the world will be poorer - and less amusing - without them.

I set off for the far side of the park. As I approach the trees, just about able to see the enclosing wall beyond, a little girl in a yellow dress runs by, pursued by a puppy. To my right, the mother concedes defeat, stops running, and moves to prevent either of them exiting the park by the gateway I see behind her. She flicks her gaze toward me. Her eyes widen and she looks away quickly. I nod to her as I pass by, pretending not to notice as she steps away from me.

Yellow dress. There was a woman in a yellow dress last night.

I pause. No, that is the whole snippet. I shake my head, flick my cigarette butt into the undergrowth, and exit the park.

The road outside is narrow, lined with terraces that overlook the park. Cars are parked nose to tail as far as I can see in both directions. This street is unfamiliar. Where did last night's entertainments take me?

A thought occurs to me, and I re-enter the park. A brisk walk around its circumference eventually brings me to a public toilet. To my surprise, the inside is passably clean, and there is hot water. A short while later, I emerge with straightened clothing and with all outward appearances of being involved in mayhem removed. The grimy filleting knife I found in my pocket has been deposited in a convenient wall cavity revealed by some anonymous vandal's efforts.

I hear the sound of early morning traffic and decide that returning to the quieter back streets confers no advantage. Exiting the park by a slightly wider gateway, I find myself standing beside a decent road, with pavement on both sides and businesses fronting on to the path opposite. Looking about, I see a sign for a roundabout to my left. Unable to discern the words, I walk toward it.

They become clear a few minutes later. Eastbourne? What am I doing in a stultified resort on the South Coast? Never mind. A sizeable town will have certain things that appeal to me at the moment. Firstly, charity shops for a change of clothes. Then shoe shops - if the charity shops cannot provide. Followed by a café, as I am famished. After that, a railway station.

I follow the directions on the sign and head for the town centre. The screech of tyres, as a garishly painted hatchback accelerates hard off the roundabout, makes me turn. The driver maintains control and it shoots off in the opposite direction to me.

Screeching. A fading wail. A rapid series of images crash through my mind. Last night contained many similar noises.

And then the memory is gone again. I resume walking, lighting a cigarette as I go. Another pause, as I consider the words on the matchbook: Elliot's Bar. The number underneath has an unfamiliar dial code. At some point last night I was there. Or was I? The place triggers no memory.

I search for clothing first, and a charity shop supporting Cats Protection is the winner, being the first of three stores that accept card payment. Browsing the books as I make my way out, a hardback copy of 'The Collected Plays of William Shakespeare' catches my eye.

A play. I had been at a theatre. The woman in the yellow dress had been on stage.

Shaking off the memory, I move on to seeking food. It doesn't take me long to find a 'greasy spoon' off the main thoroughfares that likes the look of my card. A full English breakfast with a lot of sweet, black coffee to restore me. As I gaze raptly into my second mug, memory nabs my attention once again.

I had been drinking coffee at the theatre. After that, I had been on stage with the woman in the yellow dress. Then a blank. Then the turmoil of flashing images and screeching.

Progress at last. I have breakfast, and a sequence for last night. I set to and wield the knife and fork with little flourishes that make the old boy sitting at the table by the slot machine grin. I grin back, then pause.

Grinning. I saw myself grinning, the much longer knife in hand. I was looking in a mirror. Backstage. Last night... A murder mystery! I had been involved in an undergraduate production, no doubt for an old people's charity or some such, and it had been upstairs at Elliot's Bar in Eastbourne.

The rush of memories, as a reward for guessing the plot, is not forthcoming. Obviously, I am missing some salient details. I shrug and finish my meal, supplementing it with a further two cups of coffee. Standing outside, savouring a leisurely cigarette, I consider what I know and decide that it will all come back to me eventually. It's time to find the railway station and start my trek home. After I've recalled where exactly that is, of course.

The streets are getting busy. I wish that I hadn't mislaid my watch and phone, but they're always the first to go. Suddenly, I know that there is a box with a half-dozen of each back at my flat. I walk on, enjoying the fresh breeze and the sight of people doing what people do. I'm feeling relaxed. It must have been a good night.

A very good night: in memory I see a woman mounting me. She has a purple dress rucked up round her hips. Where this fits into the chronology, I have no idea, but the memory makes me smile.

Then a builder wolf-whistles at a woman walking down the opposite side of the road. With a tingling shock, I recognise her. My memory widens its view, and I see her face watching as the one in the purple dress descends upon me. I smile, and see her blanch as she spots me. She turns right and disappears into the building site. Embarrassed retreat is nothing new – did she follow the purple-dressed one into the saddle?

I continue, crossing the road to glance through the window of a day-care home. The sight of children running about amidst the colourful toys stirs something deep inside.

Running figures. People beating on doors. The knife in my hand is large, and covered in blood.

After all this, it had only been another performance?

I brace myself against a wall as the memories sleet back: Tom suggested actually doing the play. Patty insisted that we stage it somewhere where none of our friends could wander in before we perfected it. Bruce suggested Eastbourne. His granny had lived there and he had always hated being dragged down there in his youth. Ella had bought a purple dress specially. Bruce contacted an old friend down here. She was, was – Dawn! The woman who had ducked into the building site!

Things were coming together. The Proper Cambridge Drama Society had come to this geriatric paradise to stage the first, full European production of 'The King in Yellow'. Ella had shagged me 'for luck' before the performance began - as she always did to relieve herself of stage fright. Dawn must have quit the venue after seeing me caressing Ella - with my knife - as she rode me.

Last night we had an audience of fogies and hipsters, with a smattering of Goths. All of whom had, had - what had they done? As fast as it came, it goes, taking the rest of the tantalising details with it. But enough remains for me to know that being on a train away from this town - as soon as possible - is a good idea.

I arrive at the station after only a couple of wrong turns. As I stand on the concourse, the announcer mentions a connection to Bradford, which sends my mind skipping down a chain of connections: Bradford was home to Morrisons - Morrisons had been the name of the local butcher where I grew up – which is why I always buy my knives at Morrisons.

Ah, yes. My knives.

151

The knives that had whetted themselves upon cast and audience so many times. Even when the play brought forth real artistes from the audience, it still left so many to victimise. But this time, Ella had tried to stop me, instead of bathing in sanguine excess. So I took edge to her pale skin at last, a consummation so long in coming.

Neither of us were drama undergraduates, but we had both imitated them many times. The copy of the play that Tom 'discovered' was mine. It was the only thing that gave me the means to find surcease from my cravings.

I lost it! Ella had torn it from my grasp as she slid off my blade to tumble backwards, shrieking, down the stairs into the fire we had set. The destruction of The Under Ground Theatre as a coda: reducing any surviving witnesses and evidence to ashes, as usual. Which explained my scattered recollection. The thing that maintained my sanity was gone.

"Mister Stephen Alperton? Please stand still, sir. Make no move until you are told to."

I hear the click of firearms engaging. The area about me has become devoid of people while I contemplated. It seems my days as an actor and director are about to be interrupted by those unappreciative of the arts. No matter. I can remember the highlights now that my head has cleared.

The cigarettes and matchbook had come from the body of Tom's Ukranian girlfriend; she had been the one in yellow dress. I smile as that answer finally arrives: it had been bothering me.

Then, as my hands are being pulled behind my back, the final absent memory slinks back like a scolded dog: I remember why Ella had balked at performing our usual encore.

"I'm pregnant, Stevie. It's time to stop."

Never. The show must go on.

IMPLOSION

We are Krakatau. When Mitch told us where to go, and quit the band, we all thought he'd toddle off and go back to burger flipping. Next thing we know, he's got together a four piece outfit and called it Anak. I was livid. Anak Krakatau is the native name for the volcano growing in the ruins of Krakatau's caldera. It was sheer arrogance, and galling, for him to name his band that!

The gigging scene round our way was pretty intense. When it came to flavours of extreme metal, we had been at the top of the stack for ages. The only thing that kept us from the big time was that the other guys in the band considered it a hobby. Two self-released albums and an EP that all got reasonable reviews. We were all but made. Okay, there were a few haters, but what did they know? My vocals were in the vein of classic Manilla Road, with the power of Slipknot. Annoyingly, 'Friday night pub imitators' was the sentence that ended the online review that was most circulated. I tried so many times to get it taken down, or replaced with the one I liked, which had the lines: 'metal for serial killers' and 'vocals like Satan's pissed at you'. It didn't do any good. The British curse of looking for the worst in anyone who dares get up and have a go at doing something arty, I suppose.

Anyway, there we were, making good money - and me always pushing for the guys to get off work a bit earlier so we could do gigs elsewhere. South Coast metalheads were poorly served for gigs; we could make a killing, and increase our following.

Next thing I know, bloody Anak are doing a 'Beachhead' tour. Playing small venues in coastal towns, all round the country. Starting in Brighton! Just because their bassist was the bloke who wrote the songs that made his previous band a million after he quit, they got preferential treatment. I picked up the phone and gave Mitch what for. He just laughed. Told me that the lads wanted to keep it a hobby because they knew I wasn't good enough to cut it in the big leagues. I hung up.

As they say: 'don't get mad, get even'. I spent days brooding over what Mitch said. Then I had an idea. Like Queensryche's classic line-up, we'd do a concept album that would blow all of the bastards away, and launch us into the big time. Pete, our guitarist, was classically trained, and taught guitar. He'd be able to do some fancy arrangements. All I had to do was come up with the concept and the songs. I started searching horror and occult websites for something that hadn't been done already. An extreme metal concept album would have to break new ground. I went backwards. Old stuff. Like Poe, but stranger. That was the ticket.

Late one night, I came across a track called 'Dim Carcosa'. It was a moody track, damn near spoken word. But it had something. I checked out Ancient Rites, the band that did it, but it was a one-off.

So I followed the name Carcosa and sure enough, there were a few articles from the eighteen- and nineteen-hundreds about the place. A few other groups had done related stuff, but nothing epic.

That did it. I went into it seriously and bought a load of stuff from a games company who seemed to have the goods on all of it. I read the lot, as soon as they arrived, and thought it was all a bit trite: not even remotely what I was looking for. Then I saw hints on various forums about a banned sourcebook. A play entitled 'The King in Yellow'. That was more like it. But I couldn't find the bloody thing. Nobody had a copy, or weren't owning up to it if they had. I had the broad outline and did some basic stuff from that, but I needed the real thing to get the songs done. After making a lot of enquiries, I resigned myself to waiting.

One evening, after a gig, some bloke came up to me and asked if I was the one asking about 'the play'. After a bit of back and forth, he said that he'd found a battered photocopy amongst his dead dad's stuff. Had the same title. For a couple of hundred quid I could get it off him. I went straight down the road and maxed out my credit card. A couple of hours later, I met him again and handed over a roll of twenties. He gave me a thin wad of A4 paper in a plastic wallet. It had the right title. I looked inside and… the words! Oh man, the words. This was the stuff, alright.

I spent all night reading it. Epic. Really epic. The next day I copped a sickie and stayed in to write lyrics. They were amazing. We were made. Sometime in the evening, I rang round the band and pitched my idea. I had the goods to make an album that would set us up better than Metallica. We needed to raise interest, though. I said we should stop gigging for six months and then come back with a big concert, with full-on 'shock and awe' pyro, and do the whole new album live. They sounded a bit off, but I talked them round to it.

So I settled down to read the book again. I had the entire first act broken out into lyrics, now I needed to do the second act. Maybe I could write enough for a double album, one for each act. Get some artist off the net to do a weird art piece for the cover: maybe some sort of fold-out. Yeah, this was going to be a classic.

I started the second act just before midnight and, by five in the morning, I had it. The greatest metal album ever written. They'd beg me for the secrets of how I did it, but I'd just smile. We'd be huge. I'd be worshipped; the second act changed everything. I rewrote the lyrics for the first act to bring them into line.

But then a thought occurred to me. What if they hated it? This was banned. Maybe they wouldn't be ready for it, couldn't handle the insights I laid out? Then it would be back to the Dog and Runnel, back on the circuit. We'd watch other bands make it while we stayed as the metal band you knew would always be playing somewhere, just because it was Saturday night. Always in the wings. Maybe after we disbanded, some metal god would mention that we inspired him. That would be it. Our moment of glory: a mention in some bastard's memoir. Some spotty-faced little metal kid in clean denim and creaky-new spiked wristbands would ask me for an autograph on a second-hand copy of one of our CDs. They'd sell for a fortune on the collector's market - but we wouldn't have any left to make anything from.

By then, the band would have settled down: Pete would be tutoring in the States, Max would be married with four kids and a house in the country, Rob would be off doing something cool in Hong Kong or Dubai. I'd be stuck with the echoes of what we could have been.

Why bother? Why not just do what we did and make some money, have some fun, and nail the odd rock chick too new to the scene to know that we were also-rans? Maybe I could get back with Karen. Those had been good times. Maybe I should see if she could put up with me when I wasn't spending all my time trying to be a metal god. That was a good idea. I liked that. Someone who gave a shit about me. Thinking about it, she'd been the only one. The rest didn't care that I wanted to make it. They just wanted to make money and have fun. Why did I bother? All of the lugging, and hassle from promoters and venue owners, who needed it?

Tomorrow I'd give Karen a ring. Just a quick one, so I didn't seem too desperate. I was, but hopefully she'd be nice. I always liked her, I just didn't see that life mattered more than the little bits of fame I could scrape from pub floors. Actually, it was never fame. It was notoriety. Christ. Would she even want to speak to me?

I'd find out tomorrow. Get some kip first.

The lake is still. Upon its shore stands a bare-chested man in leather trews, his long hair blowing in the wind. His features are cast in stark white and ebon shadow by the light that filters across the sable waters.

Defiant, he punches a hand toward the grey heavens and shouts something unintelligible. Then he covers his face with his hands and falls to his knees, shuddering in the grip of a dreadful epiphany. As it works upon him, he rocks back and forth, crying inconsolably.

He is naught but a transient; I know his type. What he sees here will change him, like it does every spirit that visits my realm. But he will be one of those who flee. His delusions cannot hold.

VADE MECUM

I'm waiting nearby when he arrives home. There is nothing that I do not know about him or his habits: from his current - supposedly ideal - home life, to his estranged ex-family, and the acrimonious divorce that caused the estrangement. From a stalled career, to the monthly rendezvous with an Oriental prostitute: furtive, hasty, oral, and never with the same girl. His wife suspects, but as she is in a long-term affair with the head of his department, it suits her to maintain the status quo.

Three months have passed since his call reached me, through the various channels it had to traverse. In my line of work, extreme caution is the only way to ensure that I continue earning. There are organisations and individuals who have dedicated themselves to removing my kind from society.

He exits his car and looks about. He is wondering if his request made it. He is wondering if the payments he made, from an account unknown to his wife, have attracted attention. He is worried. That is a good sign.

I settle down to sip on my peach-flavoured water and wait a while longer. Wednesday night is the only night when his entire family goes out: the wife to 'Pilates', the twins to ballet and karate respectively. Time and timing: they have been the masters of my existence since this duty fell to me.

Five years ago I was a vagrant, fallen at last from dropout into the dirty underclass that is one step above a beggar accepting the pitying tag of being 'homeless'. My family, such as it was, had been comparatively wealthy. I had grown up in a stable home, free of any childhood trauma. Sometimes I wonder if that is the reason why, as soon as I was afforded a measure of self-determination, I tossed it all away in an orgy of everything venal, feckless and stupid that I could plunge into. Theft, drugs, extortion: the whole gamut left me with physical scars, but my mind was untouched.

My mother once accused me of having the morals of a snake. I smilingly replied that a snake had no morals. She stared at me until I understood that was exactly what she meant.

In amongst the grief I pulled down upon my family, only my grandfather seemed to ignore it, welcoming me whenever I dropped in, usually to hide from something or someone for a few days. His council flat - high in an inner-city tower block that was riddled with every malaise that you'd expect it to support - made for a fine sanctuary.

We sat up late, night after night, talking about the world outside and the people in it, using terms that would have got us both committed, had our conversations been witnessed. I never really paused to consider just how psychopathic my grandfather's advice was. It all seemed to make perfect sense.

Eventually, my ability to create trouble for myself forced me to move away from home. Shortly after that was when I became a vagrant, and, after barely six months, I knew that I would die without a drastic change in my circumstances. So, in a desperate attempt to avoid my end, I walked a very long way through a cold autumn night to arrive, sick and stinking, outside my grandfather's door. It was past three in the morning, but I beat on the door's sheet-metal veneer without consideration.

Nothing happened for a few minutes, then, without warning, the door swung wide. My eyes tracked from the pistol levelled at my head, to the steady hand, to the tanned arm protruding from a quality shirtsleeve, and stopped at the darkly glinting cufflink.

My voice quavered: "Granddad?"

"Good gods, Bryce! I nearly put your lights out. Get in here, boy." He recoiled at my state: "You smell like something that should have been cremated. Straight into the bathroom with you. Get clean, and everything you're wearing goes in the bin liner I'll get from the kitchen. Move!"

His last word cracked like an order, and I tottered into the bathroom. It was dawn by the time the cooling of the bathwater I had been drowsing in - which was the fourth refill of the tub, and the first to remain clear - roused me. I sat up and saw a robe hung on the bathroom door, with a pair of slippers by the sink. There was even a toothbrush, still in its packet, propped up against the toothpaste dispenser.

It was a paler but revitalised me that wandered into the lounge to be drawn over to the table - that acted as the divider between lounge and kitchen - by the smell of bacon and eggs.

"Eat. Have some juice too. Then sleep; you can use the bedroom, I sleep in here."

So I did. No questions arose in my mind about my grandfather's acceptance of my state, his calm in dealing with the situation, his atypical appearance, or his possession of a firearm. The smell of hot, fresh food and pull of a decent bed with clean sheets. That was my universe, and I fell into it with grateful indifference.

I woke sometime during the day. Beside the bed were a couple of bars of something with foreign labels, a pint of water, and a folded card with the simple instruction: 'Eat Drink Sleep' written on it in my grandfather's hand. I obeyed.

The room was dark when I returned to the world, feeling better than I had done in a very long time. Fumbling about rewarded me with the switch for a side lamp. In its forty-watt glow I saw that a chair had arrived, with clothes upon it and shoes beneath. To my surprise, they fitted well. An even bigger surprise was the quality. Someone struggling to get by on a state pension couldn't have afforded these.

After dressing, I walked slowly into the lounge, where grandfather was working away on a very modern-looking laptop. As I entered the room, he raised a hand, to indicate he needed a moment, before pointing toward the kitchen: "Coffee. I take mine black with four sugars."

While he finished whatever he was engaged in, I made coffee. More correctly, I poured it from the jug that stood under the percolator.

Fresh coffee? The mysteries were beginning to overcome my numbness. Something about grandfather didn't add up. I put the coffee next to him, and he looked at me with a knowing grin.

"You've worked out that all is not what it seems to be, with me."

A nod in reply was all it took. He stretched his legs and put his feet up on the coffee table. Sipping his coffee, he gestured for me to take the armchair. When I had settled he waved his hand to indicate the flat.

"This is nothing but a convenient ruse. If I wished, I could live in any of the most expensive boroughs in London. But if I did, it would only be a short while until I suffered a fatal accident."

He looked at me, but I had no comment to make. Nodding in approval, he continued: "So here I am, wealthy beyond belief. I live modestly and no-one I know socially, except for you, has seen this aspect of my life. What I do may best be regarded as a calling. My grandfather introduced me to it, and he was introduced to it by an acquaintance he served with during the war."

His eyebrows rose at my expression of curiosity: "Which war is of no matter. I provide a service. I believe that I am not alone in doing so, but I am sure that if there are more, there are not many of us. With the rise of the internet, what we did became redundant - until a few years ago, when something happened to the World Wide Web, and to every computer system that could be used for the purpose. That event, engineered by gods alone knows who, made my work essential once again. It is work I think you could do, because you have the right outlook. The rules are simple. Never sample the merchandise -" We both grinned at that - "And never betray what you do to anyone. In exchange, you will become something beyond the usual, amongst the sheep that think they are people. You will gain immunity from many things, because of friends in high places, and gain substantial monetary reward. With which you can buy whatever you like. There are no limits. Interested?"

Of course I was. I nodded.

"I need to hear you say it."

"I am interested in learning to do what you do."

He smiled: "Good. Put simply, people make contact with me, and I deliver something to them. They make a copy of it, then I depart with the original. The thing in question is this."

He reached down by the settee and lifted a slim binder into view.

"This is one of the very few copies, in English, of a work entitled 'The King in Yellow'. It has strange effects on anybody who reads it. For that reason it has been banned, either openly, or by tacit agreement between governments. The latter situation being the one currently in force.

It has to be taken to people, because electronic copies stored or accessed on any device will be subtly altered to render them insipid. This even applies to copies on DVDs and the like. Whether what you see is what is actually on the disc is a moot point. Someone, somewhere, did something very clever and spread it all over the net. So, physical copies are all that retain the impact of the original."

I raised a hand: "What makes it so effective?"

Grandfather shrugged: "I have no idea. It is so dangerous that you dare not read it. After I retire, when I get bored of enjoying the wealth, I will read it. I have promised myself that. The one thing I ask of you is that you shoot me after I have read it."

That shook me. The look of calm determination in his eyes. The absolute clarity of purpose. It was spellbinding, unavoidable. I wanted to be whatever he was, to have that level of conviction, to have the hidden wealth. To have that answer to childhood cravings: a real super-secret thing.

From that night onwards, I worked with my grandfather. I learned the methods for verifying a request for the book. How to avoid being noticed by those who sought to restrict access to the book.

In a country where surveillance is king, the art is to not be noticed, rather than striving to be invisible. Little things, like dressing correctly, and displaying the correct mannerisms for your clothing and location. Being at ease in any environment. To make sure that your client uses a photocopier that is not connected to a computer. And, should the unexpected occur: to be able to draw fast from a concealed holster, kill with the first shot, then escape the scene without leaving a trace.

The application of very old skills to this new, digital world was fascinating. When our opponents can detect devices used to avoid detection, if detecting us does not work, it made sense to do away with all of them. I have not carried a personal electronic device for over three years.

I took over grandfather's work two years ago, just after I got my own - unremarkable - place, and he has started to hint that he will be needing my final service soon. Which makes tonight's client visit all the more appropriate.

The wife departs with the twins, and the street is quiet. I am sure that he is not part of a snare operation. He is just a man who needs something more than the hollow thing which his life has become. He craves something, and having been unable to satisfy that craving via the usual methods, he chose to look further afield. Friends gave contacts; contacts gave leads. Those leads led, by a circuitous route, to an anonymous internet drop-box. From there, the request eventually made its way to me. I vetted him, while he paid a substantial amount - in instalments - without hesitation.

Tonight, his dreams will be answered. I cross the road at a medium pace: just an agent for something mundane, making an evening house call upon a client. Nothing to arouse suspicion.

The doorbell chimes. The face I see when the door opens has aged.

"Good evening. I'm from Thale and Castellan. You requested a visit to review your situation?"

He blinks. Then my father's eyes widen: "Bryce?"

I smile: "You can call me Herald."

THE NETS WITHIN

During the day, this place is infested, with seekers of facts about life, and those seeking - if only for a little while - to escape from their lives. As the day sinks into the dark blue tones of evening, in that gap between the commute home and the traipse out to seek diversion, this place experiences an all-too-brief moment of invigoration.

People used to instant online access seem bemused by the quiet, the expectation of browsing by moving bodily between walls of collated and trapped words. No matter that their homes are likely to have materials from the same family within them. Here, the wood has attained a higher state. A previously venerated state that, like all objects of reverence, has fallen in regard as new ways are found that deliver the content whilst eviscerating the ritual.

As a child I read a lot: forced into seclusion and inactivity by the malady that I inherited, which sieved the nourishment from the air that I breathed, denying my body the riches that every other child took for granted. I grew pale and thin, until medical science gave me the means to clear my lungs. In response, I became determined to surpass what I could have been, in the fraction of my childhood that remained.

But it was too late. My mind had become accustomed to being diverted into the contemplation of higher things than the flesh required. My teens were split between bouts of sporting activity and periods of seclusion, the need for which would descend upon me without warning, producing a panic-ridden compulsion to retreat from social pursuits into the isolation of my room; be it at home, in a hall of residence, or the precious environs of my first flat.

In the end, I had to compromise in order to survive in the adult world. My flat lacked a settee, but had the finest treadmill I could afford. From there I could peruse the various media channelled into my home, or read one of the many books mounted upon the adapted music stands that were affixed to the sides of the treadmill's frame.

The idea of presenting a book through other media fascinated me. Adaptations of books in any form drew me. Films were frequently disappointments: presenting the barest content of the book, severed from the heights that the prose within had attained. The stage presented me with a dichotomy: works regarded as classics were presented, by and large, unadulterated. Every word was regarded as sacrosanct, and omissions were treated as verging upon blasphemy. Recent works seemed to suffer for this, as frustrated directors savaged them to compensate for being unable to wreak their vision upon the classics. The occasional reworking of a classic surfaced, but by and large, the delineation remained. 'Adaptation' had become a dirty word for audience and critic alike.

Disappointed, I returned to my temples: the libraries of Britain. There I revelled in the divergent and subversive views presented, the gamut of human emotions, the perversions and psychoses delved into. The written word has one advantage: to impose censure, one must have those prepared and able to navigate the material involved. The sheer volume of books published permits a freedom of expression that remains unadulterated across the decades. Television, and similar, has been brought low by the manipulations of those with agendas, be they societal guidance, greed, or a combination of the two. 'Opiate of the masses' is polite obfuscation. 'Diversions for the stupid' would be closer to the truth.

A closed library is the playground for creeping silence. It seeps out to nip at the heels of those who confine it for the night, and frolics unnoticed behind the backs of departing staff. When the last door closes and the beeping countdown of the alarm is stilled, the silence burgeons into a roaring thing. It romps the aisles and leaps the desks, prodding gleefully at the blank screens of quiescent computers. I have listened to it reclaim its domain so many times that it seems like a friend.

But it is not. The silence has traps familiar to me, nets of what-was-that-noise and did-something-move that clamp down upon your breathing. If you let them close fully, your lungs will gasp for air as your sight blurs. The movement glimpsed in your darkening vision will be the silence rushing in to steal your breath and ravage your mind. It is a hungry thing, and how can it not be? These places are built on knowledge. People have come here for years, seeking greater understandings. Every opportunity to add to the knowledge available must be taken. Your thoughts and memories can be sifted for nuggets that can be added to that sum.

I survived my first purging. Since then, I recognise its approach, and breathing disciplines, learned in my childhood, stave off its attacks. Constant vigilance is needed, but it is not onerous after it has settled to being habitual. The monies spent installing complex security would have served better in the purchase of more books. A library is quite capable of protecting itself.

The aisles each have a character under the rule of the roaring silence. The books stand like tenements and the pages are like things and people within them. Each isolated, yet in close proximity to neighbours they have never exchanged anything with, bar brushing acquaintance as a page turns and settles. Each aisle hosts an unmoving town upon its shelves, and manifests the *Karas* for it: a realisation of the mythical 'spirit of place' that all locations blessed by the visits of living things eventually attain. It is these *Karas* that give character.

Fiction aisles are capricious; although the horror, war and science fiction sections are best left unprovoked. History aisles are like distracted, elderly teachers who seem incompetent and dithering - but from whom you learn the most. Engineering aisles are deadly serious, but possessed of a wicked humour that extends to the fastenings of your clothing and the mechanisms of your accessories. The information technology aisles are filled with mutterings and nonsensical whimsy. But your devices may improve, or stop working, after your visit. Sports aisles are bluff and cheery, yet can turn into something more terrifying than the horror section without warning. And so it goes. I know these places and they know me. We are all denizens in the domain of the roaring silence, and we each know our place.

It took me many weeks to gain access to the Rare Books section here. Within the metropolis that is the aisles, this place reminds me of a cross between a luxurious retirement home and a bleak sanatorium. Aisles of portentous self-importance or refined elegance stand alongside those of screaming deliria. The Banned Books section here is, without doubt, the most magnificent assemblage of broken treatises I have ever visited. The aisles are small and frequently the inmates are locked within glass cells, for my safety. That being said, I have dared discovery to come back here for a second time because of what I glimpsed as I first fled: a shade. I have never seen an aisle exhibiting visual characteristics: emotions, sounds, and attitude aplenty. But colour? Never before.

Here it is, shrouded in the subtlest of bisque hues: a tiny aisle with its own glass cell. There are only a dozen books in residence, and all bar one are in languages unknown to me. I feel that while language is essential, properly mastering a single one is the work of a lifetime; I am still learning English.

What is the singular anglicised dweller in this place? A slim volume with the title rendered in gold: 'The King in Yellow'. Could this be the source of the jaundiced aura that pervades this aisle? I must find out.

This aisle has a keypad. How very inconvenient, yet simultaneously thrilling. Such extreme measures. The incarcerated must be blamed for heinous deeds. As such tend to be judged by the standards of their day, it is time for them to be paroled. A beautifully illuminated, original translation of 'The Count of Monte Cristo', devoid of Victorian censorship, will be the means of their release. Its heavy binding and brass clasps make it an ideal improvised hammer.

The crash of glass breaking is drowned, by the howl of an alarm, before the shards finish falling. A disappointingly prompt response. I shall decamp to my haven, in the triangular space afforded by the old wooden shelves of European Medieval History aisle, rather than attempting to escape. Tomorrow I can walk out: just another visitor departing.

I take two other volumes: the thinnest. My rent is due, and they should realise sufficient for the arrears, and maybe stretch to an advance as well. The silence has been beaten back by the lights and sirens, so I race between the aisles without care and secrete myself just as the front doors open. Lifting my feet onto the cross-members of the old shelf unit, I wait for my breathing to quiet. The broken latch on the old window in the upstairs toilets should cause them to think that I have fled. After all, it had been my intended route.

They are loud and busy for about two hours, then they decide, as I hoped, that the felon has escaped using the jemmied window. The head librarian seems very concerned that 'The King in Yellow' has been taken. He is reprimanded by an unknown speaker for even daring to retain a copy, and the unspoken implication is that he will lose his job for doing so. What masterpiece of forbidden literature have I liberated? How have I not heard of it before this moment? There is nothing else for it: I shall read the work before I depart.

The roaring silence is eventually permitted free reign, as they conclude that the library is safe from further defilement. I wait an hour, but it seems that no aspects of investigation or procedure have been omitted. Struggling free of my confinement, I move quickly to the reading lounge. There, in the corner furthest from the windows, I turn on a reading lamp and shade its luminescence with pages torn from a magazine. After taking time to sup a cup of water, I repair to the chair, starkly shadowed by the directed light, and open my prize.

A play. In two parts. The intersection of written word and performance, in prose form. I am intrigued. The prose is brilliant, and words I have not encountered for many years are used herein with an ease long absent from modern works. This is a gem. The first act is almost banal, but the cleverly understated hints, of portentous things to come, are delicately wrought. They draw one inexorably to the revelations that must fill the second act, as the landscape and characters are fully and beautifully described: I have joined this fading court of arrogance and intrigue, which struggles to come to terms with its sudden irrelevance; all brought to life by the words of an anonymous writer at the height of his craft.

The second act is as far above and beyond the first as Shakespeare is to a children's book. The inevitable tragedy - and the very futility of striving against the pageants that time orchestrates - crash through my perceptions. My world is forever changed: an achievement that is delivered only by the greatest of books.

My attention is drawn from the final page to the silence about me. The darkness, outside the cone of light I sit within, is thicker. The aisles are gone. They must have sidled away as my attention was captured by the book. The roaring silence has waited patiently for me to falter, for my attention to waver.

I feel the hissing quiet scatter burrs in my breathing, and flinch as the cords in my lungs snap taut. There is no place I can move to: my limbs are leaden with inactivity where the book pulled me down. If I could draw a decent breath, I could lunge forth from this trap. But the silence has waited too long for me to evade it so easily. I must... I must...what? I must have air! All else is secondary to the next breath. I hear, and feel, the wet wheezing that has replaced the clean, sure note of drawn breath. I struggle to focus, as childhood panic rears from what I thought was its grave. Like all things you lock away in your mind, its incarceration has only made it stronger. My fingers are trembling as they claw at my collar, an instinctive reaction against strangulation that happens even when, like now, my neck is free of constraint. The air. It tastes so sweet in my mouth, yet the nets have tightened too far. I reach for something. Anything. Succour, I beg of you.

There is nothing there but the silence, waiting patiently for my demise, for an end to my rude intrusions into its domain, in the most final way imaginable.

My sight is blurring and my limbs have become remote, unresponsive things. The light fades, and the darkness sweeps in. As vision dims again, I know that I am probably sinking for the last time; then the darkness turns to a shade I know and fear.

The ending begins, and I am lying on my parent's bedroom floor once again, listening to the silence after my mother's last rattling breath. Her final cigarette burns unfinished, and the lazy swirls of smoke rise to vanish against the nicotine-stained ceiling. That is the shade that surrounds me.

Fear goads me mercilessly. With a gurgling, wheezing sob that forces spent air from my lungs, without hope of replenishment, I see again the unfocussed nicotine dark beyond the lamplight. In that hazy expanse I glimpse an attenuated patch of sulphurous yellow: like someone standing upon the fringe of the roaring silence's domain, watching me asphyxiate.

Perfidious Counsel

"The play is not based in reality. Nor is it allegorical, Mister Stephens. Put simply, it induces a detrimental state in the reader, in which the reader's own doubts and fears can overwhelm him. There is some discussion regarding it being a meta-meme that causes a state akin to that experienced by sufferers of acute post-traumatic stress syndrome. At best, reading it will lead to a psychotic break. The worst outcomes are classified, and have been for many decades."

"Classified? How can people going nuts be classified?"

"Apart from the considerations of doctor-patient confidentiality, I presume that some of those involved were connected to official operations that it is not in the best interests of national security to draw attention to."

"Why haven't I read about this?"

"Again, I am not privy to that information, but I believe there to be an unwritten agreement in place at international level."

"So this is censorship by stealth. The public are not being allowed to decide on the potentially revelatory contents of this work, because certain important people fear the possible outcome."

"I do not think so, Mister Stephens. One thing I do know is that the body of evidence regarding the harmful nature of the play is vast. Many of the original sources have no vested interest in stopping a simple two act play, about a degenerate royal court, being read. What possible motive could there be?"

"The play pertains to the less-than honest origins of the House of Windsor. There are damaging secrets concealed within it. If people can identify the characters and situations portrayed, the resulting exposé could destroy the people of Britain's belief in the Royal Family's right to rule!"

"Cooper, please. You know I must caution you right now. That sort of tabloid sensationalism is entirely inappropriate. And that is apart from the fact you told me the play predates the formation of the House of Windsor by twenty-two years."

"Please don't take me for a fool, Miles. Two decades is a negligible period for the schemes that run our so-called free society in the west. The play is allegorical, sure enough; that allegory relating to the shenanigans that surrounded German royalty taking the throne of the United Kingdom before the First World War even ended!"

"Calm yourself, Mister Stephens. Your interest in conspiracy theories is well known to me – it is, after all, why you were referred here - and while I am quite taken aback by the scope of what you suggest, I put it down to the fact that you are incapable of seeing this any other way. That being said, I must emphasise that in this particular case, you are entirely mistaken."

"I'm not. We'll see who has the last laugh, when I start an internet campaign to get the play released from this conspiracy of silence so experts can review it properly. Today's attempted 'intervention' will feature highly, I can assure you."

"Cooper. Please do not do this. Your continued psychiatric care programme will be set back by this."

"My company is paying the bills, doc. Work it into your programme and charge accordingly. Better make sure you get your money before this all comes out, though."

"Mister Stephens –"

"We're done, Doctor Wheeler. See you in the funny pages."

The door slammed behind Cooper Stephens, and Miles Wheeler sighed, removing his glasses and massaging the brow of his nose to relieve the pressure he had felt building during that final exchange.

Dammitall, he liked Cooper. But the man was a combination of brilliant investigative reporter and full-tilt conspiracy nut. That mix was potentially catastrophic when applied to the situation regarding the play. He would have sleepless nights over what he was about to do, but some things went beyond doctor-patient privilege - and personal preference as well.

Picking up the phone, he smiled as he dialled a fourteen-digit secure line number without pause. This was only the third time in eighteen years, but the fearful memories of what he had seen and read still ensured that the number was always instantly recalled.

"Prognosis Twenty-Eight on Cooper Stephens."

The voice at the other end sounded concerned: "Are you sure, Miles?"

He sighed: "I would give everything to be anything but sure, Daniel. Twenty-Eight is confirmed."

"Shame. He's a fine reporter."

"I know. But his hobby is about to become his new campaign. The pitch is that a cover-up conspiracy about the founding of the Royal Family is concealed within the play, which was written in 1895."

A short chuckle presaged the reply: "Well, well. A new barmy theory. Thank you, Miles. I would wish you a good weekend but I know you'll be blaming yourself."

"Thank you, Daniel."

Miles replaced the handset and rubbed his closed eyelids with the heels of his palms. Then he pressed the intercom and asked Ella to go and get him a coffee and a Danish, along with whatever she fancied.

While she was out he could amend Cooper's notes - using her system, so records were seamlessly maintained. He would also schedule Mister Stephens for an appointment next Friday.

Everything must be as if the clinic expected him back as usual, no matter that he'd be dead before next Wednesday, killed in an accident that had absolutely nothing remarkable about it whatsoever.

A DECISION OF MY OWN

The decisions of my days are terrible in the consequences of me making the wrong ones. But if I make a mistake, it will be bad, yet I will see her. How much more can I stand of this dichotomy?

I want to see her but I do not want the bad. In the end, I retreat into the me that has been taught to behave, shutting down the me that used to run laughing through the rain.

It is a sunny day.

He will go to the pub after work.

I will start his dinner an hour later, so it will be ready when he comes in.

Better not. He could come home to see if things are right. If the dinner is cooking, he will want to know why it was started late. That would be bad.

He will shout at me about his dinner, but not much.

I will put a beer in the fridge.

Better not. He will want to know who I had it in the fridge for. Who did not drink it, as it was still there when he got home. That would be bad.

The dinner goes in at the usual time. The beer stays in the box in the pantry.

I watch some television. Everyone seems to know the secret that nobody told me. How to have a man like the ones in the films. Someone who holds your hand when the two of you are alone. One who makes love with a smile, and makes you close your eyes and cry out little noises of pleasure. One who wants children. One that laughs when you adopt a puppy, instead of drowning it in the sink.

The front door swings open, and I am halfway to the kitchen when he arrives there.

"Where's dinner?"

I stare at his shoes: "In the oven." I use mouse-voice. It does not work. The slap spins me to slam against the sink.

"It's no use in the bloody oven, is it?"

I rush to serve, making gravy to moisten where the meal has sat in the oven for three hours too long. He looks sourly at the plate, then at the gravy in my hand. With a single move, he throws the plate across the kitchen, and twists my hand so the hot gravy pours down my dress.

"Stupid woman. Look what you've done! Go and clean yourself up."

I shuffle past him and out of the kitchen. My down-cast view sees the lump in the crotch of his trousers. That's bad.

The shower is barely warm, because we have to save money. I rub myself hard, trying to dry off and warm up at the same time. My robe is thin but I like the primrose design. It is one of the few things that belonged to the time before him, to the me who ran in the rain. In the bedroom, I drop the robe and grab for my baggy nightshirt, but I am too late.

"Ready and waiting? Good."

He grabs me and bends me forwards over the back of the chair. I hear his zip and hear him spit. This is very bad.

It is, but it is over quickly. He barely has time to thrash me before he finishes. Withdrawing with a grunt, he marches into the bathroom, whistling. I have learned to stay put. When he comes back, he laughs and takes me suddenly. I make the smallest sound of pain. His laugh deepens, and it gets very, very bad.

Afterwards, he kicks me and tells me to clean up. When I try to stand up, he slaps me down and tells me to crawl. So I crawl to the bathroom and cry into the flannel. If I use the shower again, he will thrash me for wasting water.

I creep onto the bed and curl up on the edge. He grunts, but lets me be. It is cold, and I am naked, but trying to put my nightshirt on will get me beaten for disturbing him, and he might decide to do things again.

The dream comes quickly, like it always does after bad times. I'm nude and swimming underwater - or a drowned ghost. It makes no difference here. She is next to me, face showing concern as her hand rests on my bottom.

"He hurt you again." It is a statement.

I nod.

She shakes her head: "It does not have to be. Mine did to me what yours will do to you, and I was so afraid. I screamed and water came in and my eyes burned and my ears hurt. Only afterwards was I free. Join me. Take your freedom: rise from this place."

For a moment, it seems possible. Then I shake my head. So we swim, and smile, and turn somersaults in the warm black water. Even though it is black, I can see the ruined city below. The stacks of the city still smoke, but I don't know how - we are underwater. A dream is all it is.

With that thought, I am back on the edge of the bed: cold and afraid to move. By morning, I am stiff from the chill and the bruises. I make his breakfast and endure his attentions, then he is gone. I wait for an hour before being sure.

Then I run a hot bath and slide gratefully in to it. There I sleep, stirring only to get myself a coffee in one of his pint glasses. Me who ran through the rain makes me smile and stretch, makes me use his razor instead of mine. Little acts of defiance are all I have.

He returns early, and wet, as his car broke down: my fault for making him forget to do something at the weekend, because he was distracted by having to thrash me for hours. I had bought new underwear. He thought the elegant garments, that I spent so long carefully selecting, looked like something 'a slut' would wear. So he gagged and tied me with them as part of the lesson.

It is another bad evening, but he doesn't want to do things because I make him 'want to puke'.

When I ask if I can go for a bath, he only grunts and opens another beer. I take that as a yes and retreat upstairs, lock the bathroom door and run a tepid bath like I am supposed to do. I float in the water, looking at the ceiling. My ears are submerged, so I do not hear him coming. The door flies open, and his hands are on my shoulders.

I go all the way under.

Flailing arms find his razor that I forgot to put back on his rack earlier. I take it to his face and surface to the sound of him screaming. This is very bad.

But I don't care.

The barrage of blows begins and, for the first time ever, I fight him. I scratch and bite and kick and slash with the razor. There is a lot of blood and, for once, it's his. Then he hits me with the soap dish. I feel myself topple back into the bath as my consciousness falls apart.

The darkness in the water swirls as she swims around me.

"You are back soon."

"I fought and he hit me hard. I fell into the bath."

Her brow furrows: "A time of choosing is coming. But I will always wait."

I smile, grateful for even a dream friend.

I come round, as he tenderly wipes my brow with something damp.

"Silly girl, you mustn't do things like that. It makes me angry."

Looking up, his face is covered in a patchwork of poorly applied plasters. I try not to smile, but can't. Luckily, he thinks it is a smile of compliance.

"Good girl. I'll put you to bed. Tomorrow we'll do something special."

He does that and only that. No doing things, or pushing me off the edge of the bed 'by accident'. I sleep quite well.

The waters are dark, but we are near the surface, I can see lights from one side. She is with me again, hand on my shoulder.

"That is where we can go when you arrive."

I smile and shake my head: "Why can't we go now?"

She reaches up and raps her hand on the underside of the water's surface. It sounds like wood.

"We are in different states. When you are the same as me, it will not be like that."

We look the same, but she knows this place better than I.

I smile at her: "Can't you be like me, then?"

She spins about, arms outstretched: "I was, and will never be chattel again. His word is bond and his word to me was of a match for my soul. He will do the same for you, after I introduce you, and if you ask."

"Who is he?"

There are steps above. I see two walking figures, one in trousers and shirt, one wearing a shapeless ensemble that could have been fresh from gamboge dyeing: its colour was so pure.

She points at them: "He in raiment to match the lights is he of whom I speak: my liege."

There is something strangely alluring about this: the freedom of the water and the promises of what awaits above. If only this were not a dream.

Next morning he is cheerful. It makes me nervous. But he insists that we are going somewhere special. Then it starts raining, and his guise slips.

"Into the car. I hate driving in the rain."

That is because he drives too fast, thinking he owns the road. I rush to get ready and throw myself into the car as he puts it in gear. With a squeal of tyres, we are accelerating before I get my seatbelt fastened. I clip it in, as he laughs in contempt. He never wears one.

The road is awash, as the cloudburst hammers down. Details are impossible to discern through the windscreen, yet we careen out onto the dual carriageway. Coming off the first roundabout, the car skids but he brings it back, swearing at me for dragging him out in this weather.

At the second roundabout he tries to cut around the outside of an articulated lorry. For a moment, I think his crazed driving will win out once again, leaving nothing but a scare and his laughter. But this time is reckoning time. The wheels of the lorry skid, as the driver brakes hard after seeing us too late. The water on the road is greasy, and the back of the lorry snaps sideways before its tyres grip. What looks like a wall, made of hubs and tyres, slams into our car like a cricket bat hitting a ball.

His scream is a falsetto shriek as we catapult off the road, up and over the verge, through the wispy trees, and drop into one of the fishing lakes. We land with a splash, and skate a little way in a spray of water, before the car settles with a foreboding gurgle.

He opens his door and scrambles out. The inrush of water slams me against the passenger door, and I feel my fingers snap where they were trying to undo my seatbelt. As the car starts to sink, I hear him call to me and see a hand thrust through the opening opposite. It seems so far away.

"Grab my hand. Cat! Grab my hand!"

Even in this, he tries to command me over a decision that is mine: to continue a life spent in futile attempts to avoid his wrath, or to see the whole of my dream. It is my choice. With a rush of warmth, I realise that me being able to choose is his greatest fear. So be it. Closing my eyes, I loose my grip on this wasted life. I feel the car dip as he leaps off, and it does not bounce back. The water is cold, and I hear ducks before I go under.

She is there, arms spread in welcome. I smile shyly. I'm nervous.

"You decided." Her brows quirk: "Have you decided?"

I nod and feel my smile blossom. A weight lifts from my soul: "Yes. I want to rise. I want to meet your-. No; our, - um...?" My voice trails off.

"Liege. Take my hand."

With my hand in hers, we rise, and pass through the formerly solid surface to stand upon it as if it is a floor, rather than the vast black lake I see it to be. My attention is caught by two moons rushing overhead, and my mouth falls open as I see the black stars above them.

My companion prods me to get my attention, then waves toward the beautiful city before us: "You see? He waits upon the jetty. We are expected."

I hesitate. What does this mean for me?

She tips her head to one side, as if she heard my thought: "You have woken. From now on, decisions about you are yours alone to make."

With a smile, she stares pointedly: "Although the first should be about what to replace that with."

I look down to see that I am dressed only in my primrose robe. Next to the impossibly fine dress she arose from the waters wearing, it is a rag. But I am the one who ran laughing in the rain, and I will keep it - for it kept me.

I gesture to myself: "I'm Catrina."

She catches my hands and moves them aside, then embraces me in a fierce hug: "And I Calandra. Shall we sally forth and introduce you?"

I nod and we set off, hand in hand, toward the imposing figure in the yellow robes. He regards us with eyes like pits of night in his pallid face. As his tall crown cants slightly with his nod of acknowledgement, a fading part of me screams; but all I feel is safe.

By Moonlight, All Things

The wave crashes over the city and I wake, shivering, in the light of dawn. Every night since I heard her sing it has been like this: a marvellous, ancient city overwhelmed by an impossible tide. I hear the people scream, and masonry crack like cannon, as the wave comes down with a sound so monstrous I have no words to describe it.

Nothing I do can shake me from the grip of that dreamscape. It is as if my dreaming self has taken residence there, while my waking self mopes around Paris by day and night, a target for venomous words from the locals that I do not understand, yet can so easily grasp the gist of.

It was an evening like this, but under a gibbous moon, when the shackles upon my soul drove me, like some hapless heifer, down to *Parc Montsouris*, across its broad expanse and down to the corner abutting *Rue Nansouty* and *Avenue Reille*.

Upon my approach, as if to order, I heard those three lines carrying on the clear air of a summer evening, to the accompaniment of minor chords strummed upon her guitar.

"There is a city, far away -
Where night did rise,
Instead of day."

The rest of the song was sung in a French dialect that sounded stilted and old. She told me that her name meant 'Dart' in English. Apart from that, we shared no language, bar a few common words, gestures, and pulling faces at one another. Laughter featured a lot as well but, although it brought us closer, there was little understanding involved.

I was desperate to find out the meaning behind the song, but she only managed to communicate that she had learned it, including the English opening lines, from her grandmother.

And so we whiled away the nights, moving from café to café if we were ejected from the *parc*. Her accent or dialect was unpopular. People shunned us. When they found out that I was an Englishman who did not speak French, the contempt escalated, and we moved on.

That night, with starts and glances, we wound our way across the city to shabbier lanes and brooding, dark alleys. Dogs barked and music played from windows above. Dart's manner changed. Her carefree walk turned into a furtive creep, and she frequently waved her hand for silence. Twice she dragged me into the shadows, as groups of tough-looking young men sauntered by.

Finally, we came to a little house set back from the road, the gap between the two filled by a burgeoning vegetable plot. I smiled, thinking Dart had brought me home. I was surprised when she knocked upon the door instead of unlocking it. A shadow fell across the curtain, it twitched, and then the door was opened by an old woman brandishing a gigantic revolver in her tiny fist. A rapid exchange of words followed, before the older woman turned to me.

"*Dard* says you are sweet and English. She says you want to know about the song she sings, the one she learned from my mother." She stood to one side: "*Entrer, par votre volonté.*"

Dart smiled and waved me in ahead of her. I had to stoop to get under the lintel and enter the impressively small home. Over in the corner by the open fire, a cot with ruffled bedding was crammed up against the wall. To my right, the opposite corner to bed and fire, a kitchen area sported a tiny table and two small chairs with tall, narrow backs. In front of the fire, two armchairs nestled so close they should have been a sofa. On the stove, a kettle whistled.

"Tea, young man?"

I nodded. Dart slipped past me and leapt onto the cot, provoking stern words from her grandmother. Chastened, she sat demurely in one of the armchairs, propping her guitar against the outside wall, only a handbreadth away from the padded left arm of the chair.

"So, I am Marie. Do you have a name?"

"Ted."

Her lips pursed: "Would that be Edward or Eduard?"

I smiled: "Eduard, Madame Marie. Eduard."

"Very well, Eduard. Take the seat next to *Dard*, and I shall use the cot. Then we shall drink tea like civilised people, because *Dard* brings them home so rarely. You will tell me about yourself, and I will answer *Dard's* endless questions about you. Then we will talk of the song, the city, and *Dard. Bon?*"

I nodded assent, and, in short order, we were arranged as planned and I was spilling my guts under a merciless, gentle, smiling interrogation accompanied by aromatic tea and Nice biscuits.

Finally, Marie and Dart relented. I did not know how much time had passed, but the end of my quest was at hand.

"And so, Madame Marie. The song?"

She sat forward and her eyes flickered in the firelight.

"It is an old song. My mother learned it from her grandmother, and she from her mother, and so on. Most *les Français* will tell you that it is about the fall of Ys, but it is far, far older. It tells of a young woman, abandoned by her fiancé in the city threatened by that dread tide. The 'night that rose', we think, was a wave so high that it blotted out the rising sun. As the wave began to fall, the young woman was grabbed by a man on a horse, and they raced the falling doom to reach high ground, making it by the slightest margin. Upon reaching that safe ground, the brave horse expired beneath them. The young woman, distraught, wept for their noble steed while the man, terror turning to anger, berated it for failing. Over the corpse, they had a raging argument. The man stormed round the steed's body and went to grab the young woman; whether he intended to console her or to discipline her is a fact lost to time. She struck at him and they struggled, then he lost his footing and tumbled back into the seething waters behind them. She remained by the horse's body, crying and damning the man for being a fool. It was she who composed the song, and the three lines in English were originally sung in the language of the man's homeland. Why they were changed is another thing that has not come down to us.

For her entire life, she thought about him, about what would have happened if she had only understood that it was fear that made him rage at the horse, not arrogance. She hoped he had survived, and that they would meet, even after she bore a daughter of her own by some other man. But it was never to be. She is said to be the founder of our family. The city they fled was a place strange and far from here, damned by the gods for the practice of foul things - some say for daring to believe that they could ascend to become gods themselves.

That horse, if the oldest stories are true, was possessed, during that moment of peril, with one of the great animal spirits. That is what allowed it to escape certain doom. It galloped between realities whilst its riders clung on, eyes tightly shut, expecting watery death to take them at any moment. The story says that the benediction of that spirit, for the girl's actions in mourning the horse's passing, is why the women of our family have always had an affinity for horses. Now you say your father owns a stable. *Dard* has caught herself one closer to home than she thought."

She laughed as she translated the final sentences for Dart. Dart blushed and, in response, I did too. Marie pointed at the two of us and clapped her hands in delight.

The night was wearing thin, as was my ability to remain awake. Marie gave me directions to return to the city centre and told me to come back the following night.

I staggered back to my lodgings and fell into a dreamless sleep. While I slept, a great storm raged across Paris, and scrubbed the skies clear. The following night, the moon shone silver bright as I made swift steps to Marie and Dart's little house.

For the life of me, I just could not accurately retrace a reversal of the route Marie had described. Over the following week, I counted the turns back and forth countless times, but the little house with the vegetable plot out front did not come into view. I checked the tenements about, and the angles of the taller buildings, all to no avail. The place seemed to elude me.

Visiting the *Parc Montsouris*, I was greeted with silence every time. The moon shone down and people strolled, but of guitar notes there was not one.

By the dark of the moon, I retraced my steps to the patch of waste ground where I thought Marie's house should be. As I mooched about looking lost, an old boy in shabby dungarees came up to me. When I responded to his French with English, he grinned and replied in a broken Welsh accent.

"Been a while, boyo. Been away, have ye?"

I looked at him: "What?"

He jerked a thumb back toward the waste ground: "You've been coming by since the King's moon, looking like you lost the prize of your life. Same as you do now."

I was no clearer for his explanation: "I'm sorry. I haven't the faintest clue what you're talking about."

He pulled a greasy pipe from his pocket and tamped it quick. As he lit it, his eyes sparkled.

"You met a girly because she sang a song. It drove you nuts, and you kept having crazy dreams, so you finally accompanied her home to get the story about the song from her granny. Am I close?"

I nodded, dumbstruck.

"Then you slept like the dead for a day, and ever since then, you just can't find the place, can you?"

I shook my head.

The duffer reached out and patted me on the shoulder: "You been visiting back a-whiles, boyo. That little house stood here until nineteen-eleven. Then they levelled it off, because of what happened: they said no-one died in the big flood of nineteen-ten. Ask the locals about that. Plenty died, but no-one deemed worthy of reporting. That little place? It housed an old woman and her granddaughter, who made their living singing songs, telling tales, and selling vegetables. The big flood went through the foundations and the place settled hard. Didn't collapse, just settled enough to block the doors and windows while it filled with water."

My throat had turned to parchment and I croaked as I waved my hands. Then I pointed at the sky.

"Yes, I know that's impossible, boyo. I've been here forty years trying to prove it, and find her again. Leave me to it. Get on with your life. It's what Dart would want you to do."

I sat down hard and waved frantically at the moon, then pantomimed a crown upon my head.

The grizzled oldster knocked the dregs of his pipe out on his boot-heel, then crouched down by me.

"The King's moon is a funny thing. I only sees that particular moon when she's about. Or maybe it's t'other way round. Only see her when it's about. Never figured that out to me own satisfaction. Anyhow, legend tells of a king named Talbar, or something like that, who offended the gods so badly that they sent the seas to destroy him, his city and his people. But the king and a woman survived. Seems that another king, a golden king, one way more popular with the gods, did for him in the end. Then that golden king created a vicious curse to make sure the descendants of the woman who escaped drowning all died as she should have."

By that point, I was shaking my head slowly, whether in denial or disbelief, I couldn't tell.

The old boy nodded: "Yes, I thought it was all rubbish too. But that particular yellow moon is called the King's moon, and I seen the house a couple o'times by its light and none other. But it's gone by the time I get close. Just the *noyade cour* like you see tonight."

We both turned to regard the empty expanse of dirt and rubble.

Finally, I found my voice: "What does that mean?"

He looked at me, the sparkle gone from his eyes: "*Noyade cour?* Pretty sure it means 'drowning yard'. Go home, lad."

The wave crashes over the city and I wake, shivering, in the light of dawn. Every night since I heard her sing it has been like this: a marvellous, ancient city overwhelmed by an impossible tide. I hear the people scream, and masonry crack like cannon, as the wave comes down with a sound so monstrous I have no words to describe it. And no way to escape.

Three Sheets

The shop-door chime rang, and the elderly gentleman looked up from his brightly lit tool bench. His eyes narrowed as the visitor was silhouetted against the glare of the streetlights, becoming instantly recognisable.

"I told you before, I will tell you again. I will not make it, in any form."

"Mister Greaves, my boss says he will double his offer."

"He could multiply it by a hundred, and I'd still say no."

The door closed, and the figure moved nearer, the clean lines of a handsome face interrupted by a ragged goatee beard. The face split into a huge grin.

"Kurt, you said the same thing last time."

Kurt Greaves smiled up at the young man: "And?"

Nick Lassiter pulled his hands from behind his back, revealing a brown takeaway bag, straining at the sides, and two large teas: "You said if I asked again, you'd tell me why."

Kurt slapped his desk and barked a single cough of laughter, before pushing himself back to stand and look up at Nick.

"You have grown again."

Nick put the food down as he shook his head: "Nope. Still six foot seven. You've got smaller."

Kurt grinned: "You are probably right. All these schmucks coming in and asking me to make jewellery with forbidden glyphs. It wears a craftsman down, all that evil."

Nick paused: "Evil?"

Kurt moved to sit behind the counter. He grabbed the bag, talking as he unloaded it: "Only by the results, and usually by the nature of the people who ask for it in the first place. Like your boss, Nicky."

Nick wagged a chopstick at him: "Low blow, *Herr* Greaves."

Kurt looked pained: "*Herr Ehrlichmann*, or Mister Greaves. Mixing them up is *peinlich*."

Nick shrugged: "I'll take your word for it. So, why won't you make the pendant for his nibs?"

The older man sighed: "If I do not die or disappear after completing it, your boss may – although that would be no loss. But if he manages to give it to whomever he intends it for, I would be party to murder."

"Murder?" Nick's complexion paled. He knew his boss was no angel, but he thought that Crem Dresner had genuinely gone legitimate.

Kurt may as well have heard his thought. He pointed a chopstick at Nick: "Going legit is not becoming lily white overnight. How do you think those big businesses survive all the harm they do? They may appear clean, but they hold the leash on many who are not. That is what Cremaj has done. He has finally learned how to play the big game in this city."

Nick wrestled with that whilst idly gnawing on a sweet and sour rib. By the time he dropped the bone into the bag, he'd concluded that Kurt was right - he'd only been fooling himself.

"Good point, Kurt. So, my boss is setting a lady up. Makes my skin crawl, that does."

Kurt smiled: "It says well of you that it does. Now, do you want the story?"

Nick nodded.

"It starts a long time back, and a ways away. We are in Pforzheim, at the edge of the Black Forest, in my homeland. The year is 1855. The man who owns the jewellery shop with the window of tiny panes in gold-painted frames is Reiter Goldschmeid – he was the last of a line that had worked with gold for so long it had become their family name.

The story goes that Reiter was wondering if he could continue. The arrival of machine-made jewellery, and the increase in artisan jewellers, reduced the profit he could make on each piece, to the point where it barely covered his expenses.

Into this scene of woe comes a Prussian gentleman, a classic of the breed. He says that Reiter had been recommended to him by one of Reiter's old patrons. He says that he requires a *goldschmeidemeister* - master goldsmith - because he has a masterpiece that needs making.

Reiter is flattered. He asks after the health of his former patron and then - carefully, you understand - he broaches the subjects of deposit, crafting time and cost. The Prussian gentleman laughs and places a wooden casket before Reiter. When he opens it, Reiter sees a fortune in cut and uncut gemstones. All this, the Prussian says, is yours if you make my masterpiece. Reiter doesn't hesitate. The fortune in the casket would secure his future. He asks if the gentleman has the design for his piece to hand. The Prussian produces a wad of vellum. On those pages is a simple gold ring with a single dark stone in its setting. Upon that stone is a strange pattern. The gentleman goes on, at length, that the pattern is shown across several pages because it must only be complete when engraved upon the stone and inlaid with the purest gold.

Reiter does not heed his own doubts over the commission. The value of the gems is far beyond what the piece would cost, even beyond what it could command if sold as a completed piece. He decides that if the Prussian wants to pay that much, then the gentleman has his reasons, and it is not for Reiter to question such providence. So Reiter accepts the casket and the papers, tells the gentleman to return in two weeks, and sets to work.

Ten days later, Reiter is found dead in his shop. Nothing has been taken. There is not a mark upon him. The casket of gems stands beside the designs for a ring. Obviously a commission, but the patron never comes forward to claim his fortune. As the ring is nowhere to be found, it is concluded that, obviously, Reiter had not commenced. This is despite two local gold merchants swearing that he had purchased quantities of pure gold from them the previous week, and used gems in payment. Gold that is nowhere to be found in Reiter's premises."

Kurt pointed at the edge of the folded papers protruding from the inside pocket of Nick's coat.

"Look to the plans you carry, Nicky. The glyph will be spread across three sheets. It always is."

Nick did so. The pendant and chain had a page apiece. The pattern Kurt called a 'glyph' was detailed, in parts, across three pages. He looked at Kurt, questions writ plain on his expression.

Kurt shrugged: "That story is only the first. Across Europe - and from America, since the First World War - the same tale is passed amongst the makers of bespoke jewellery. The glyph on three pages is deadly. Some take the job and survive. Most do not."

Nick looked at Kurt: "What about the ones who survive?"

Kurt nodded: "For this story, we must visit the Chicago of Al Capone. Mike Gresnau was the jeweller. He makes the piece - yet again, a ring - and hands it to the man from Duke Neadham, a minor gangster who wanted to be Capone.

Duke gives the ring to the man who runs the allied gang, Reeferman Tom. He was a moonshine runner and had a reputation for bringing 'southern hospitality' to gang warfare. Hangings and burnings were his trademark. So when Reeferman Tom is found dead, only a few hours after getting the ring, his ignorant and superstitious lieutenants conclude that the ring must have been poisoned in some way. They burn Mike Gresnau in his shop, with his family in the apartment above. No-one survives."

Nick tapped his finger on the counter top: "You're saying that the glyph thing can never be used for anything except getting people killed?"

"Yes."

Kurt watched as his young friend did some fast growing up, right before his eyes. Finally, Nick straightened his shoulders.

Kurt pointed at him with a pancake roll: "A decision has been made, I think."

Nick smiled: "You think right. I think I'm going to take a certain Miss Amelia Turvell on holiday. A surprise one. Involving a lot of changes of destination and cash payments."

The old man smiled in happy surprise and waved at the empty tinfoil containers: "This means we will not be noshing the Chinese for a while?"

Nick nodded: "I'll drop you a postcard. It'll say it's from your granddaughter. The picture on the front will be where we've ended up."

"What about your boss?"

"He'll find a fool to make the pendant eventually. I won't be his delivery boy, but I'm not his only henchman. So I have to take his target away, and disappear myself. Plus, old man Turvell will be a damn sight better at saying no to whatever Dresner wants, when his daughter is not available to be used as leverage."

Kurt clapped his hands: "You are a good man, Nicky. Luck to the pair of you."

Nick stood up and smiled: "I'll need it. She's going to hate me."

Kurt reached out and shook Nick's hand: "Only at the start, my boy. Only at the start."

HEART'S ABYSS

In the room next to the office, visible through an observation window, an unusually pretty young girl, dressed in threadbare casual clothing, was laughing in wonder and disbelief. Her companion, a slightly older girl in obviously brand-new casual clothes, was demonstrating a games console: something the younger girl had plainly never seen before.

Watching from the office were two people: a grey-haired woman leaning heavily on an ornate cane, and a woman in well-worn street clothes, her dreadlocks hanging almost to her waist.

The older woman gestured to the two girls: "Susan's playmate is Edith. Edith has been isolated from mainstream society since birth. This is all a huge adventure for her, with wonderful surprises at almost every turn. She is a delightful child with a keen intelligence and a surprising level of education."

Cara Thwaite saw Edith flick a glance toward the upper corner of the room: "She knows that she's under observation. How much of this is an act?"

Ms. Carlisle hobbled painfully back to her desk before replying: "That is one of the problems. Edith is everything I have said, but she may be more. Finding that out will be one of your tasks."

She reached down and retrieved a bulky folder from a drawer: "This is your set-up file. Everything is covered. You and your adopted daughter have just moved into a house in a pleasant, quiet residential area on the outskirts of Hove in East Sussex, an area filled with professionals who commute. Very few questions will be asked."

Cara watched Edith flick a glance toward the observation window and smile. It was a welcoming smile. Then Cara felt the chill she always got when someone unseen was watching her.

"Miss Thwaite. I should mention that you received this assignment against the wishes of every member of the selection panel. I overruled them. I feel that your experiences while working undercover, when combined with your recent loss, will be advantageous, rather than an impediment. That being said, I should caution you that if you fail, my favour will turn into the ill wind that kills your career."

Cara smiled: "I will not fail. Edith needs a surrogate mother and, quite honestly, I need someone as well. Something that you knew already, I suspect."

Ms. Carlisle nodded: "Any questions before you start?"

Cara returned her gaze to the observation window: "What was Edith rescued from?"

"A cult. One deemed to be a threat to society."

"What happened to her parents, and what does she know about it?"

"Her mother went missing two years ago. Her father was a fatality during the operation that liberated Edith. Her view is that her mother went to a place called Carcosa, and her father has gone to join her."

Cara looked back at her commander: "That's it?"

"Acceptance of bodily death as nothing more than a change of state for the consciousness is a core tenet. You die; you go to Carcosa."

"Another afterlife paradise?"

"No. A place where souls can spend eternity becoming better at being themselves." Ms. Carlisle looked up and smiled: "That's the best our phenomenologists can come up with. The emphasis placed on self-determination is, however, unusual. Not one member of the cult was actively recruited or coerced."

"Doesn't the United Nations have rules against attacking that sort of society?"

Ms. Carlisle smiled: "An astute observation. Technically, we attacked a rural commune whose only transgression was to hold an odd set of beliefs. What we did was morally unacceptable when viewed from the perspective of public ignorance. The inhabitants of Roshannor had the misfortune of being devotees of the most socially entropic threat ever encountered. I was horrified at the very idea of tasking the SAS Special Projects team with performing such an attack, until I was briefed by those who deal with this thing for a living. Then I was terrified."

Cara raised a hand: "There's a unit dedicated to whatever inspired this cult?"

Ms. Carlisle fixed Cara with a cold gaze before speaking with careful emphasis: "Not even one to handle the psychologically damaging literature and deadly manifestations. Are we clear?"

Cara responded with a sharp nod: "Silly idea, ma'am. Please excuse me."

Ms. Carlisle nodded: "I think we're done here. Dismissed."

As the door closed, Tabitha Carlisle slumped in her chair before turning her gaze toward the observation window. Edith stood by it, looking toward the door in Carlisle's office. Then, with a shout, she spun and rejoined her companion, just as Cara entered their room.

Cara thought that putting the two of them in a four-bedroom detached home was a disgusting waste of taxpayer's money, but who was she to complain?

"When did he die?"

Edith may as well have crept up behind her and hit her with a bat. The unexpected query tore through her carefully wrought calm. Cara felt tears spill down her cheeks as she spun clumsily, gasping for air, to confront the girl.

"What did you say?"

"I asked when your boyfriend died, Cara." Edith was matter of fact, sitting on the bottom stair with legs crossed, looking just like a typical girl, asking questions, about something of which she should have been ignorant, in the tones of a woman many decades older.

Cara swallowed a couple of times: "Ten months ago."

"How did he go?"

"He stepped in front of the train he usually caught to come home. No one knows why." Cara had spent weeks trying to answer that very question, finding nothing except heartache and breakdown.

Edith smiled: "He died well."

The praise in her voice was genuine. The words were so antithetical to what she expected that Cara found herself sitting on the floor as her legs gave way.

"How can anyone die well?" She choked the words out, as sobs abetted her tears.

"He chose to leave. Nothing made the choice for him."

"So he chose to leave me, his family and his friends? Why?"

Edith looked straight at Cara, golden motes floating in her eyes: "I don't know. You'll have to ask him that."

"Ask him?"

"When you get to Carcosa, you can ask him."

Cara's world spun. With an effort – that, for a moment, she thought she wouldn't make - she came back from the edge of the abyss that had nearly swallowed her so many times since Tom's death.

"I'll think about it. What do you fancy for tea?"

"Can I have waffles? I had them for the first time ever this morning and they were delicious." Just like that, Edith was only a twelve-year-old.

"Waffles? I don't know if we have them. Shall we investigate?"

Tea was an exotic selection of things Edith had never tasted. Which seemed to be everything that couldn't be pulled from a vegetable patch, or dragged from pen - or field - and slaughtered.

Edith told blood-curdling stories, about mishaps when killing livestock, like they were anecdotes from a day at school. Cara was taken aback, but Edith's droll delivery soon had them both giggling.

Television was another innovation to Edith. One that she was singularly unimpressed with: "Why do so many channels show people desperate for attention?"

Cara confessed to not having an answer. Eventually they discovered a mutual appreciation of vintage Tom & Jerry, and decided that it was the pinnacle of televised entertainment.

It was gone midnight when Cara called time, and they headed upstairs. As Cara sorted out Edith's room, Edith washed up and donned a worn nightdress patterned with sleeping teddy bears. While she brushed her hair, she watched Cara from the bathroom doorway.

"Isn't it difficult to comb your hair?"

Cara grinned: "It's impossible. To care for this lot, you keep your scalp clean and use a technique called palm rolling."

"Did he used to do that for you?" Edith's tone had changed. The woman in the girl had returned.

Cara bit her lip, trying to use the pain to avert the wave of grief that threatened to overwhelm her. Only partially successful, she trembled, and tears started to fall.

She whispered: "Yes, he did."

"It must be hard without him."

"Dreadlock care, or life in general?"

"Both."

"I get by."

"I don't understand. You miss him; you know where he is. Why not go there?"

Cara turned slowly and stared at the girl, seeing the golden specks in her eyes again: "Edith, I don't share your beliefs. For me, he's gone, and nothing can bring him back."

"That's sad. No, it's wrong. I know he's there."

"And I know he's not. He chose to go, but it wasn't a good thing he chose. He chose to abandon those he loved. That can never be a good thing to choose."

Edith thought about it, then smiled: "So, when will you see him again?"

Cara sighed: "A part of me says never. Another part says after I die, he'll be waiting."

The woman-girl pondered before saying: "So even you are unsure of your next journey."

Cara sputtered: "Journey? It's called dying. You stop journeying."

"No, you start. Just like you journeyed before you became you. When your body dies your soul will go on, to come back as someone else."

"Reincarnation? That I don't believe."

"Neither do I. There is no higher purpose, no balance, no growth. That's why people go to Carcosa: to stop."

Cara felt the abyss within yawning wide. How many more times could she pull herself back from the brink, pull herself back from curling into a ball and never coming out?

Edith pressed on: "You must choose to go. Waiting to die is too late. You cannot let time decide for you."

Cara's vision swam: "Let time decide? I suppose that's true. In the end, everything we do is decided by time."

The room seemed darker, as Edith leant forward: "What if that were a lie?"

She was losing her grip. She could feel her carefully built mental barriers crumbling under the assault of an impossibility she so badly wanted to believe. A battering driven by the beguiling arguments of something that looked like a twelve-year-old girl

Cara gritted her teeth: "Time is something no-one can oppose."

Edith's beaming smile was a beautiful thing to behold, until Cara realised the girl wasn't smiling at her.

"Time," said a voice that seemed to come from far behind her "is of no consequence."

Edith leapt over Cara's wilting form with a shout of joy. Cara heard only three light footsteps before the silence of solitude descended about her. She knew she should drag herself into her bedroom and press the panic button, but a part of her argued - quite rationally - that she was not panicking. She was calm, like a convict about to accept the resolution of a death sentence.

Something brushed against the door frame. The distant voice came again: "A moment of choosing is upon thee."

"Choosing between what?"

"To wake from your dream or to remain."

"Is he there?"

"Alas, not yet."

"Yet?"

"He has your heart?"

Tears fell like running water: "Yes."

"If you are there, he will surely come."

"Will that be soon?"

"Time is of no consequence."

"You mean that?"

"Yes."

"What do I have to do?"

"Choose."

Cara wiped her eyes and only blurred her vision further: "I can't see where to go."

"Look to your darkness."

Grateful for permission at last, she curled into a ball on the floor, squeezed her eyes shut, and slipped over the edge of the pit that held her grief.

"See the light."

Howling pain and raging sorrow funnelled her toward a void of loss. But, at the event horizon, golden motes spun slowly, in almost stately fashion, describing a pattern that seemed to define a somewhere in the nowhere of her collapsing noesis. Cara felt her distant body smile as she plunged, laughing, into the cage of golden motes.

"Come away."

The motes spun faster, and she felt herself shift. Gold turned to black and slammed backwards, to become stars, in negative, against a sky that was the grey of the darkest thunderheads. As her perceptions reeled, the impossible sky was replaced by a vaulted ceiling, inlaid with silver filigree that shone like captured moonlight

212

in the radiance from thousands of candles, and many less identifiable forms of illumination.

She fell upon deep-pile golden rugs, the tiny patterns worked into each thread hurting her eyes, until she lifted her head away.

Rolling over, while her body shook, she searched by gaze alone, taking in the splendid fitments of the gigantic hall she lay in. Indistinct figures clustered in the shadows around the edge of the place, rich garments only hinted at by the reflections they gave.

Looking behind her, she saw a throne carved from a giant yellow gemstone, which held a greater lustre than any jewel she had ever seen. Midway up the flight of gold-edged ebon steps that led to that throne, she saw a figure in yellow robes moving with stately grace.

Her voice seemed jarringly loud as she asked: "Edith?"

The figure paused upon the topmost step, but the familiar, distant voice still seemed to come from beyond where - he - stood: "Inherited belief is not choice, and a child is unburdened. This place is not for those without burdens to shed by choice."

Cara stood up and looked at the throne room about her: "Where is this?"

"You know."

She did.

STORM WARNING

Dear Mr. Marsh,

As requested, this letter and the document that accompanies it are the only record of my study. They have been hand-written - also as you requested. (As an aside, it was quite refreshing to return to penmanship.)

Your organisation has collated a wealth of material, but as far as I am aware, my study is the first to look at it holistically, using data-mining and similar deep-analysis techniques of modern derivation.

What follows has not been included in the main document, for reasons that will become clear. I will admit it was with a profound shock I realised that I needed to write the following for your sole attention:

AN ADDENDUM TO THE CONCLUSIONS WITHIN

'A RE-EVALUATION OF THE DOVE-GRANT TREATISE'.

The evidence and results will undoubtedly be analysed in tedious length by many. Therefore, I will step past what is already documented to offer a personal interpretation.

The sheer volume of entries displaying a consistency of reported elements cannot be disregarded. Themes are easily transmitted: colour (yellow), distinctive apparel (robe/mask), unusual locations (lake) and environmental peculiarities (rapid moons/suns) etc. Emotional content is not so easily passed on. Yet throughout the testimonies, it is actually even more consistent than the themes.

Analysis of past emotional environments is for historians. I shall restrict myself to the twenty-first century. The primary reason for people's susceptibility seems to be an almost nihilistic desire for the near-insurmountable pressures of living in today's world to cease. Symptoms can be characterised as a need to find sanctuary - to find a place where you can just be yourself - without having to justify or understand your psyche, your partner/family, your choices, your devices, your failings, et al.

The secondary reason seems to stem from what may merely be a deep-seated refutation of the primary reason. Denial, marked by a compulsive drive to dominate/own/master this ultimate, nebulous 'thing' that so many crave.

Distinguishing which 'reason' is applicable is quite straightforward but, unfortunately, a post mortem event (of the mind at least) in most cases.

Primary Type One

One of these will occur:

1. Permanent vegetative state.

2. Sudden adult death syndrome.

3. Physically goes missing, sometimes in what could be categorised as impossible circumstances.

Primary Type Two

The victim becomes dangerously psychopathic, usually in multiple and/or layered ways, which inevitably leads to death or detainment, with all detained sufferers lapsing into catatonia on their first night of incarceration. Death will occur within a few days, regardless of medical supervision.

NB: The collateral damage caused by a sufferer in the active phase of this state is notable for the scale and cunning with which it is inflicted. I would characterise it as 'a vengeful malice toward human society in general'.

<u>Secondary</u>

The sufferer is found dead with occult paraphernalia all about and, occasionally, an incomplete copy of the play nearby. It will be obvious that a ritual of some kind had been in progress.

With the rise of the maladies collectively referred to as 'burnout', the mental state that makes a person susceptible to the play is occurring 'naturally' in more and more people. (The instances of 'sane' people reading the play and promptly departing from sanity - and sometimes this world - seem to be falling. Information overload has its uses, it would seem.)

While your organisation's actions have effectively barred the original version of the play from the net, I see evidence of deliberate and targeted physical distribution. That needs to be stopped, quickly and permanently.

How would your internet sentinels cope with a streamed live performance of the play? If, as I suspect, the genius who did the coding has gone the way of anyone who ever performed an in-depth study of the play – namely, hopelessly insane or dead - then you have a problem.

What about impromptu street theatre and similar 'spontaneous', or short-notice, public gatherings? For example - how about a 'flash mob', each given a line to recount, performing the second act en-chorale on the concourse at Waterloo Station?

I trust that you see where I am going with this. Attention-seeking fools could do it, but any fanatical group with even a smattering of occult knowledge could realise the potential at any time.

You cannot continue with the strategic expectation of remaining covert. If a 'mass reading' occurs, you have to be able to override COBRA etc. for effective response and aftermath handling.

And now for the 'intuitive' leap:

You mentioned that someone once said to you "there has to be more to this than just a play". That someone was right.

Primary reason sufferers go to him/it.

Secondary reason sufferers call him/it to them.

By extrapolation, he/it has a vicious temper when called.

Behind the legend lies a truth (that may be a clichéd line, but in this case, I believe it to be wholly accurate). I am sure that the 'King in Yellow' is an entity of unknown nature and purpose.

NB: While his/its actions may seem malignant, in the light of cold analysis they are revealed to always occur in reaction to initiation by human agency.

What to do about him/it? I don't know, except to say that I believe regarding him/it as a physical entity, and thus a target for removal, would be a grave mistake. If he/it actually exists, then he/it lives somewhere a long way away, and far beyond the borders of current (and foreseeable future) science. This is one bogey that no-one should send Squadron F after.

I could go on, but my sleep has been troubled enough of late. Please do not hesitate to contact me if you need clarification or further input.

Yours sincerely,
Hugo Niebure.

P.S: If my recent sleeping problems presage an unwelcome but not entirely unexpected outcome, please ensure that my family is looked after. Thank you.

Nothing Withstands

This article, neatly hand-printed on a sheet of bond paper, was found within a stack of carefully folded clothing retrieved from the south side of Clifton Brook, between junctions 18 and 19 of the southbound M1, just after dawn on December 14th 2013.

The world is his already, of that much I am sure. But he will wait. For implicit ownership is not enough. He waits for us to come to him, to make the journey his queen undertook so very long ago.

Not for him, the dreamers and the visionaries. Their lofty ideals and dramatic woes are as puerile and brief as the games of children. He awaits those who fall under the weight of the world, having experienced too much, yet not enough. Ennui slipped between their diversions, or satiation turned unnoticed to jaded apathy.

In this computer-dominated century, instant gratification leads inevitably to a longing for something more. When that ache becomes acute, his influence is felt. He does not call; he has no need. Those who yearn for the unattainable, yet undefined, cannot help their fascination with something seemingly so primal to their need.

Anyone possessed of imagination will know of the mornings when the effort of leaving home seems to require strength impossible, and the reason why such effort should even be expended remains elusive. The drives of wage and family are inescapable, but so too is the underlying bruising of unassuaged desire, that wistful burden of opportunities untaken. Man is a beast of stimulus, of selfish urge and sudden action. The mores of 'modern' life have bent him out of shape. It is that distortion which is the stumbling block of the id.

He is ineluctable. Because he is craving incarnate: the honey for the wasps of our souls. One night we will settle to rest, like as not in a place we have not stirred from for a while. As our consciousness slips down, somewhere between the dreaming realms and the delta depths, we will follow a distant melody, and with Arietis far behind, our destination awaits. Not that we will know. At best, a dream - of a darkened lake with a splendid city beyond - is all that we will recall.

And so we will wake, and the world will seem a better place. We will mingle and live and be welcomed back from our distracted state. After a time, there will come two things: a setback that bruises soul but not body, and a vision of radiant yellow. It will be an impossibly bright flower, a butterfly of luminous beauty, a luxury car passing by: always a thing of wonder or desire. The colour will remain after the details fade. Saffron will bleed into your dreams.

You will work, play, read books, see films, and enjoy life. But you will notice a distraction setting in. A hollow ring to the tones, and a brittle sharpness to the colours. Muted discords will arrive from everyday things. Slowly, imperceptibly, you will fade. Not to those about you, but within. The longing will drift forth once more.

Nothing of this will be forceful, or sudden, or gauche. It will be a thing of elegance and subtlety, of poise and gentility. It will eviscerate your other emotions, reducing them to palsied things against the one that stands untouched: never strident, yet utterly implacable.

You will be as one bereft, but without loss discernable to any but self. An actor in a world gone monochrome, where neither pleasure nor horror stirs thee. Save for shades of yellow. They produce a pang. A resonance. A hum that builds, down where that longing coils.

Then, one night, after your dreams quiver with reasonless warmth, you will find yourself upon those shores once again.

Will you choose to go to that city? Maybe not this time.

Will you join his masque? Maybe next time.

Will you wake? Maybe this time.

Nothing withstands he whom time rejected.

He will have us all.

The Last King

"But he is cruel, father. I like not his bearing or his colours."

"He is not cruel, my child. He is grieving. When you bring sun to his storm at last, you will meet the man we told you of."

The drapes drifted in the wind that bore scents from the groves across the lake. This far up, the hubbub from the roads was a muted backdrop to the cries of birds, buzzards and lynx. Within the room, a girl-child of barely seventeen summers stood with her back to me. Her shoulders were slumped, and she had the manner of a relative at a funeral, for all that she was dressed in the finest her family could provide. Her father Robardin, my First Counsellor, had flicked his beard over his shoulder as he bent to console and cajole his daughter. His attire would have drawn comment had courtiers seen him: in private, he eschewed the finery espoused by the other members of my court. A simple homespun robe, cinched with the braided belt that his paramour had made as her first year-end gift to him. He was barefoot, looked harried, and I decided to let him be. Vision of beauty his daughter may have become, but persuading her to do

224

anything she did not wish to was a work of time and endurance. I would only founder his good efforts so far.

As I straightened and turned, a maid froze before me, her eyes wide as her mouth opened to cry out in shock. A flick of my fingers silenced her, and I whispered softly as I stepped by: "I was not here, child. Say nought."

My muting charm passed from her as soon as I disappeared from sight, a sensible limitation placed upon our lesser wonderworks to prevent tyranny.

Another brick in the wall of my legend, I supposed, as I made my way to the throne room. That I, Hoseib Alur Binrothe, had been so taken by the vaunted beauty of Robardin's daughter that I had snuck in to see for myself. There would be veiled glances tonight. Muted conversations. Knowing looks would be exchanged. All to the good: those with contacts within my staff would be revealed. In the game of courtly intrigue, every moment and action counted: for all that it rarely did in real terms. But sometimes those 'real terms' could be things of mortal severity, and I had no intention of ceding my reign as yet, for all that I would give everything to have my Crysanthe back.

At that thought, my steps turned without conscious direction and I found myself back in our chambers. Her dresses, in every shade of red, still hung. I could not bear to order them taken down. Her jewellery and letters had been returned to her family in far Alar, along with her body. I had worked a day and a night to knit her rent flesh and lay preserving charms upon her. With the caravan that took

225

her home, went my heartfelt plea: Hali forefend the failing of the charms before she was laid to rest. Let her family and people never see what befell their most-beloved daughter.

It was a year-long journey back. My charms were the only ones capable of lasting that long. Robardin had counselled that we send a closed casket. I reminded him that the people of Alar regarded such as the funerary vessels of traitors and similar undesirables. Mortal insult would be taken.

The evening stole in with the customary failing of the breeze, so a silence spread that only the activities of people could mar. Which they always did. Talking and shouting and being so very alive, they turned the night to limited day with torches and charm-lit frames of wild shape and great diversity. I had often watched them from afar, standing upon a shadowed balcony, ruefully aware of the irony of being so reclusive, yet in a position where I could never become a hermit. Given my proclivities, a life of study and wonderworking was my calling. Given my House, a life as prince - and then king - was mandated.

As a prince, my studies had been enhanced by my position, as wonderworkers from every shore came to petition me for patronage, or to discuss abstruse elements of wonderworking and the charms that were regarded as so essential to our daily lives. As a king, the time for such esoteric pursuits was frequently absent and, indeed, frowned upon. From discussion with our foundlings, it seemed that distrust of the magically inclined was a universal constant.

Crysanthe had arrived without fanfare, as part of the tithe of foundlings from Alar. She was a red-headed young woman of lively mind, mischievous disposition and rare beauty. Those attributes were backed by a solid understanding of statecraft and wonderworking, albeit both in the varieties practiced upon her homeworld. We fell for each other within minutes, and in less than a moon's passing, she had become my paramour.

The wittier bards had declaimed that we should abandon our chosen shades for ambers upon my ascent to the throne, as it showed the merging of our lives - so obviously close had we become. Crysanthe surprised us all by composing a poem, of humour and gentle rebuke, that explained why such a merging would be wrong, as our individual natures were what would make our rule strong. At our ascension, the bards presented her with a harp inlaid with stones in every shade of red they could find. She caused hilarious uproar when she said that she accepted their gracious apology.

Against the noisy backdrop of my people's evening revels outside, the silence within returned my attention to the hall before me. I saw that the court had gathered *en masse*. Something of import was afoot and, as I was unaware, it was of Robardin's doing. Sure enough, he strode forth to stand on the audience carpets, at the foot of the sixteen steps that led up to where I sat upon the throne - an uncomfortable edifice crafted from canary diamond by Dulrothe, the first king.

There was one step for each previous monarch of *Char Kho Zhar* – which meant 'Splendid City of Gold' in the old tongue: a language that had passed from general usage during the arcane strifes that beset Ebrothe, the third monarch.

I leaned forward with a smile, and pointed at Robardin: "I sense an event of import, First Counsellor. I also sense that you are its architect. Do let us commence." I was surprised as his eyes momentarily widened and his face paled. Then he gathered himself and spread his arms. I settled myself in preparation for one of his fabled monologues.

"It is eleven moons since the paramour of our beloved liege passed, in a tragedy beyond words: the latest and the most bitter of the trials that have sorely beset the House of Rothe. We have all grieved with our monarch and hoped beyond reason for another to become the echo of his soul."

I saw many heads nod, and without apparent orchestration. A common feeling, then.

"As each moon since summer has waned, my sorrow has turned to concern. Our monarch spends too much of his time in the arcane studies of his youth, diving into familiar comforts to ease his pain."

Sharp words. A lesser man would not have dared.

"With our monarch having taken none to his chambers since the tragedy, I have been beside myself at the spread of rumours that the font of heirs has withered, but have been denied the means to decry such slanderous accusations."

The able folk of my watch-guilds had reported nothing of the sort. But, given the topic, a certain reticence was understandable.

"My creeping horror at the weakening of reverence toward the House of Rothe persisted, until my own daughter proposed a solution."

She did? Given what I had perceived earlier, that was a surprise. Robardin turned to look up at me. I could see the tears in his eyes.

"My dear Casiana offers herself to you, my liege. For one night alone, no matter what it do to her repute. To console you, to return you to the world, she would give everything."

There are moments in every monarch's reign when the experience of years combines with the regal blood in one's veins to give prescience: a seeing beyond the apparent world, into futures made likely. I had it then: a strident denial like thunder in my soul. But I discounted it. Such an offer, made by a noblewoman before an assembled court, was unprecedented. Which would explain the last-minute doubts I had heard Robardin assuaging. I was simply looking for a way to preserve my withdrawn state, and my people deserved better of me.

With an act of will similar to that of an opiate devotee breaking his pipe, I shelved my all-encompassing grief. Eleven moons was enough, because my loss would never ease, give it eleven moons more, or eleven millennia beyond that. Time to live. Time to be a monarch.

While I fought that battle, without trace of the conflict showing upon my face, Robardin waited in the breathless hush that had fallen across the court. This offer would be the breaking of his status if I rejected it. I smiled and wrought a charm of lust upon myself. As I had decided to live, reserve would be unseemly. A monarch's pleasures must be beyond the doubt or questioning of mortal men, just as his decisions and authority should be. I felt heat rise within, and my mind slid to more primal considerations.

I stood and the court dropped, as one, to bended knee.

"Hoseib Alur Robardin. The House of Ardin has always stood loyal to the monarchy. This act of selfless devotion to the House of Rothe is the crowning achievement of that august fealty. How can I deny the lady, when she would risk all for me?"

Robardin looked up and smiled. He clapped his hands, and the courtiers shuffled awkwardly, without rising, to clear a path. At the end of the finery-lined way, there stood a lithe figure in an amber dress of stunning complexity; for all that it barely concealed her, in truth. She dropped into the posture of utter subservience, with such practised fluidity that I knew, whatever eventuated upon the morrow, tonight I was going to be served well. There was no point in prolonging the preamble; indeed, the charm I had wrought made it nigh-on impossible to defer. I descended the sixteen steps and walked to meet what promised to be a source of almost certain satiation. Applause started as I passed the foremost courtiers. By the time I reached her, it was a wall of sound at my back.

She looked up, startlement upon her features but calm in her eyes. I extended my hand. Her palm was warm and dry. Her smile hinted at things I could only assign to the disports of lust, given my charm-enhanced state.

As we walked the corridors and rooms toward my chambers, I was startled. It was the first time I had designated them as 'my' chambers since she died. We entered, and I placed a charm upon the door.

There would be no disturbances from without until we were done with each other.

She stood, a statue of desire with eyes of hunger. I grinned at a sudden thought: Robardin must have spent a fortune to maintain the patent fiction that was her demure reputation.

"What is your preference, my lord?" Her eyes fell as she spoke, as if realisation of where she was had finally hit home.

"I have always been one for removing anything that conceals us, then working out what suits from there."

Her confection of a dress came away like a rosebud opening to reveal the flower. I had to know who provided that charm, but it could wait. She was alabaster. Never had I seen such white skin. Even her bodily hair was the colour of unblemished snow under a full moon. With a start, I realised that the hair on her head was coloured by charm. I flicked a nullification and indeed, her hair was similarly white, but shot with silver. She shivered.

"I said without concealment. Any and all concealment."

She nodded and I felt her release a deeply personal charm. When she looked up, her eyes were the colour of Crysanthe's blood. That thought unmanned me for a moment, then in my mind I heard Crysanthe laughing. So be it. I disrobed by charm as well. My body had weathered well, as was the heritage of Rothe. I was approaching two centuries, yet retained the body of a ninety-year-old - and a ninety-year-old athlete at that. Her eyes widened upon seeing my charm-abetted eagerness, then her smile went from distant to very close indeed.

We wrapped ourselves about each other and hobbled into the bedroom, caroming off furniture and toppling ornaments. Then, without further ado, she relieved my urgency with deft touch, which left me free to drive her wild until I rose to the challenge again. At that moment, to my surprise, she lay back and meekly offered herself to me, rather than pouncing as her previous actions had led me to believe she would. No matter. I savoured the view of her eagerness as I positioned myself over her. With a single thrust, I slid into her warmth.

I felt the charm within her resolve as I penetrated it. My loins turned to ice as my gut churned and a grand wonderworking scalded my brain. Whiteout took my eyes and a banshee screech deafened me. As darkness rushed in, I understood the reason why she had been so passive. I had to be the one to enter, to fully and willingly engage in the action, thus meeting the subtle conditions governing the charm's activation. A monarch cannot be charmed by any bar himself. This was a masterful subversion of the protections that had kept the monarchs of Char Kho Zhar inviolate for over four millennia.

My awareness came back in fragmentary images and snippets of motion. Sound took longer. Touch was the last. Smell and taste never returned. When the pieces resolved into coherency, I found myself to be a passenger in my own body. I beheld a court engaged in vigorous celebrations without compare, both in scale and luxury. With horror, I realised that I was witnessing a feast of ascension. As I was upon the throne, it had to be for a new paramour. With certainty and dread,

I waited until a movement allowed me to see who sat upon the step, at my feet. Sure enough, Casiana occupied that spot. To one side, I glimpsed Robardin, with a look of pride upon his face and satisfaction in his eyes. My first true prescience had occurred at the moment of his proposal and I had ignored it, thus becoming complicit in my own downfall.

The evening progressed as expected, with entertainers, wonderworkers, and many, many speeches. As dawn approached, I felt a touch upon my wrist and my body rose to take Casiana's hand. There were cries of approval. To my horror, she wore one of Crysanthe's dresses, tailored for her slighter form. We exited the throne room to rapturous applause. She held my hand, and I became aware of subtle pressures being applied to my palm when she needed my body to do things like turn or climb stairs. Upon entering our chambers, she steered me into the bedroom, where she stripped me, instructed me to lie upon the bed, and proceeded to pleasure herself upon my aroused state. When she finished, she left me there and put on Crysanthe's chamber gown. Moments later, a discreet knock on the door presaged Robardin entering. He regarded my supine form, lying on the inclined bed, with wide eyes.

"Do you have to keep him in a state of prowess?"

She regarded her father with a wicked expression upon her face: "Why, does it stir your needs?"

It could not be! Oh, but it could. A short while later, Casiana wiped me, as her father dressed himself, cursing as he hunted pieces of formal attire discarded carelessly in his eagerness to debauch.

"What now, father?"

"We must arrange his demise. The automaton charm is useless for maintaining life. We can tell him to eat, but we cannot tell him how to draw sustenance from the victuals he consumes. Within a year he will swell up as the unabsorbed food slowly rots. After that, his body will decompose – or, more likely, explode."

"But I must be with heir by then. How can that come to pass? I did not catch upon our first night."

"It was a likely side effect, due to the placement of the charm. But there is a way."

"I will not lie with some lackey. Or you, for that matter."

He nodded: "I suspected as much." His fingers moved fast, as he wrought a charm upon his own daughter before she could raise a defence. She stood rigid, the charm having sundered her from control of her body. Then, while she obeyed her father's command to strip naked - the trapped horror in her eyes contrasting with her increasingly obvious state of arousal - he rolled back the carpet and wrought an intricate circle upon the floor with the ease of long practice. By the time she was nude, cold grey mists from the Nether Realms swirled in the circle. With a dull hiss, a scaled being stood within. A hunched man-form falling somewhere between wolf and lizard, its manhood rose at the sight of Casiana.

Robardin turned to his daughter: "This serves three purposes. The first, to get you with child. The second, to grant me further favour with the Nether Realms. Finally, it is a lesson that you are not indispensible. I am the master of this city and you are merely an instrument of my will."

With that, I witnessed my First Counsellor command his daughter to submit to every desire of this notary from the Nether Realms, then hand her over for a merciless ravishing. After the creature departed, I thought the madness over. But no, Robardin proceeded to violate his daughter brutally, his gasped commands growing more disgusting as the night wore on. Finally, he had her mount me unnaturally, and pleasured himself as he watched our defilement. After his climax, he ordered her into the bathing room to cleanse herself.

As she crawled stiffly from view, he erased the circle then sat upon the bed next to me.

"Ah, Binrothe. The ancient wonders you missed in your studies."

His voice was quiet, even contemplative. I wondered if he knew of my aware state.

"I caught the first foundling from the Nether Realms. Returning it home gave me the introduction I needed. The House of Rothe had held sway for too long and, in you, it had reached a pinnacle of ineffectiveness. We should rule Aldones, not merely accept the leavings of lesser cities - like Alar - as tithe. Then you go and take a foundling from Alar as a paramour! It is fitting justice that he, who just begat your heir in my daughter, is the same notary who made your paramour scream your name as she died."

The rage that tore through me was unparalleled. As my conscious mind become blind to everything, my subconscious took the power proffered by insurmountable anger, and used it to sever the dependencies I had upon my captive body. This I realised as I returned from my rage, emptied of all but the barest emotion by the burgeoning need for revenge, yet possessed of a greater sense of self.

I also had a far greater clarity over my unusual situation. My state of awareness, indeed my continued existence, was nought but a freak accident. At best it was a twisted, unforeseen 'defence' wrought by my regal protections against wonderworking: as they could not save my body, they had saved my soul. Would that they had let both perish.

My view had shifted to the balcony of our chambers. It was morning. I was clean and dressed in a light robe. Across from me, Casiana sat in apparent relaxation, but I could discern the tension in her limbs, the artful makeup concealing her bruises. Without warning, she moved to sit next to me and then draped herself about me, to all outward appearances a paramour sharing an intimate moment with her love.

"Would that you were not extinguished, Binrothe. Would that the automaton spell had only been the puppetry that my beast of a father used upon me. Then we could work toward his bloody end. I cannot even command that you slay him, for he is master of the charm that animates you. I am just granted a measure of control."

Her voice was tremulous, a whispered mix of shock and profound anger. I was at a loss. I felt some sympathy for her, but the fact that she had been complicit in Crysanthe's death overreached that by a measure beyond traverse. She only wanted her father dead. I wanted them all dead.

With incredulous shock, I realised the full scope of what Robardin had had to achieve. Any who were close to me would have had to be suborned, sent away or, more likely, murdered – with suitable explanations presented for each. A slew of courtiers would have had to be set to be independent in their assessments of the kingdom's business, knowing that they could no longer appeal to me for arbitration. It went on. To perpetuate the fiction of my continued health of body and mind, a number of people amounting to a veritable army would have to be, in some way, complicit. Many would accept some excuse, rather than confront the unimaginable truth, but many more would be in it for gain. No doubt Robardin had spent years marshalling the rival Houses to his cause. In the end, the House of Rothe, reduced to only myself and Crysanthe by a sequence of now highly suspicious tragedies, stood alone.

As I contemplated, Casiana rose and steered my body indoors. Any vestige of sympathy that I held for her evaporated as she used me to re-enact some of the abuses she had suffered the night before.

Whilst my body became a puppet for vile pleasures, I remembered the old adage that said the touch of the Nether Realms was a corrupting influence. At that moment I knew it to be wrong. The corruption we harbour within is what lures denizens of the Nether Realms to us.

Weeks passed. I overheard more and more that transformed my opinion of the inhabitants of my city from tolerance to contempt. While I admitted that my state led me to place the dimmest interpretations on what I witnessed, it made no difference. If I had the chance, I would destroy the traitors, like the vermin I now clearly saw them to be.

I kept a list of the guilty until I could mentally recite the litany of names no longer. Even with my trained memory, the size of the damned host was too great. So I switched about, and found keeping a list of those I regarded as completely innocent far easier. It was also a great comfort to know that, even in the midst of my existence as a soul-sundered regicide, I could still show mercy.

One eve, I lay naked upon my bed again, the gentle slope of it allowing me to see and hear as Casiana and her father discussed my death.

"He never ventured out on the hunt. He did not even ride except in extreme circumstance." Her voice had turned shrill, as I had learned it did whenever she confronted a problem beyond her ability to seduce or have assassinated.

"True. But all those wonderworkers I dismissed have given me an idea."

Her brow furrowed: "Which would be?"

Robardin's smile turned smug: "They are a superstitious lot. They spoke in hushed tones of the evil fates that befall those who reach too far. I am minded that an accident of that nature would be acceptable."

"How?"

"Something like an explosion in his study. He had gone there to work on a grand charm - to guarantee your safety, or some such nicety. It would also remove that damnable room from this palace. It makes my bones ache every time I enter it. I swear that the tomes therein rearrange themselves when I am absent."

She shook her head emphatically: "Binrothe was famed for his insistence that grand wonderworking was always a last resort. I hardly think that he would break that reserve for such a nebulous cause as the general wellbeing of our unborn son."

Robardin looked thoughtful: "You raise a valid counter. Let me think more upon this."

The next day a reason presented itself. For 'some reason', the charms I had placed upon Crysanthe's body had unravelled, so the courier told Robardin. The court at Alar had seen Crysanthe's body and drawn a vile conclusion: that I had sacrificed her to establish a pact with the Nether Realms. Without hesitation, Alar had declared war upon us.

That night, Robardin charmed his daughter again, and let the creature from the Nether Realms take her to the very gates of death, in exchange for Nether Realms intervention against Alar. I watched him defiling Casiana's cooling body after the creature had departed. Only when he had satisfied himself did he apply charms to restore her. His earlier admission, of knowing what Crysanthe screamed as she died, joined what I had just witnessed. The result presented itself as the sickening reason for some of the insults, worked upon Crysanthe's body, which I had puzzled over but been too overwrought to investigate further.

The doubts in my soul were burned away by a cold rage. Any vestiges of regal impartiality remaining from my heritage fell before the ascension of a new facet of my psyche: executioner.

The death of my body was as spectacular as it was thorough in its obliteration. The blast destroyed the entire tower that had housed my study at its top. An unparalleled arcane library, and a life's research, turned to ashes and fragments that rained down across the city. My body was vapourised, but I remained. For a moon I hung, disembodied and conscious, where the floor of my study had been, looking down upon the palace, shuddering every time a bird flew through me. Then, with a concussion that threw me far across Lake Hali, I regained the ability to move of my own volition. By the light of the full moon, I experimented with my newly realised independence, for all that my form was insubstantial and invisible to any but myself.

After that, I travelled for years. There was nothing to return home for, until I could bring doom down upon them. Firstly, I visited Alar - and watched them burning effigies of me whilst they mobilised for war. Crysanthe had become a venerated figure, referred to as *Ehri Rei* - Red Lady. I was called *Mhsi Kun* - the Defiler. It was sobering to see the hatred. It was sad to see the power-grabbing and avarice going on, behind the noble intentions espoused by all in public. They were as bad as my former people. I departed as an army from the Nether Realms fell upon them. I presumed that one side or other would fare badly, and was indifferent as to the details, or the result.

Visiting wonderworkers became a diversion. I could feel them, if I was nearby. Despite my best efforts, I remained undetectable. I stopped trying when my situation extended an unexpected felicity: access to their sanctums and gatherings. From those, I learned many things: mostly trivia, but a few items took root in my longing for revenge – or the yearning to be reunited with Crysanthe.

They were sure that souls were a finite resource. Each one returned many times. A different life lived upon each return, with varying degrees of recall of prior existences in each case. Many showed an affinity for one world in particular, manifesting there more times than anywhere else. Strange and unexplained, despite much research, our world, Aldones, seemed to be some sort of nexus for dreaming consciousnesses. It seemed to be the one place that souls from other homeworlds could drift to. They appeared as spirits. Those spirits were immaterial unless they chose to manifest here. Presumably the body that remained upon the world of their birth would suddenly disappear, simply die, or suffer a lingering death, as the echo of its former inhabitant slowly faded.

These were the foundlings of our lands: the strangers who brought treasures of knowledge, or at the least provided cheap labour. They had all departed their homeworlds sharing common traits, which came down to a deep dissatisfaction with, or detachment from, their lives there. It was an emotional thing, of unquantifiable nature, that led them to follow the siren song of the Hyades. Unrequited or lost love was considered to be a major cause. Upon hearing that, I soared up into the void in rapture. Crysanthe would return to me - of that I was suddenly, absolutely, sure.

The revelation that the 'Nether Realms' were not another homeworld, or even another plane, was startling. They were actually a chain of islands deep in the icy north, the last remains of the sunken northern continent of our planet. The inhabitants were long-lived, thanks to their sanguine wonderworks, but they were still subject to the laws of our planet. This meant that they could die. It also raised a question regarding the 'foundling' that Robardin had 'captured'. Had my murder been part of some convoluted plot?

The origins of 'Carcosa', as their various barbarous tongues mispronounced the name of the Splendid City, was a surprise of no lesser import. The House of Rothe had its roots in the survivors of the cataclysm that sank the northern continent. Char Kho Zhar had been a territorial capitol, built to oversee a captive nation. What actually transpired was time-lost, but the entity we venerated as the aqueous monarch Hali had been an ancestor of mine, if some of the wilder theories were to be believed.

Another result, whether of rebellious sabotage or an aftershock from the cataclysm, was to create the lake outside the city that we had named for that aqueous monarch. Its darkness was due to the corroding ruins concealed in its stygian depths. Those gathered frequently postulated about what ancient wonders could be found down there, if only they had the means to survive the trek into the chill watery darkness. I, too, wondered - and suspected that the physical dangers of the aforementioned depths were nothing to my current form.

I returned to my former home one winter night, and spent a moon surveying the city. The commoners seemed to be in poor fettle, whilst the courtiers, and those who had their patronage, thrived. The half-breed monster presented as my son was growing unusually fast, something which Robardin was having trouble explaining. Casiana had acquired a reputation even her father could not quash. What I saw her doing in the stables during the dead of night caused me to flee in revulsion that took several weeks to pass.

As I returned from that flight, I passed through the poorest section of the city. Curiosity got the better of me, and I drifted through some of the hovels. It was something I had never seen: how poor people lived.

In a shack barely bigger than the floor space occupied by my former bed, a family of four made do as best they could. What startled me most was the little shrine set up by the fireplace. A crude carving of me in my flowing robes of state, wearing a miniscule tin copy of the Winter Crown, stood between two smoking candles. As they finished their meal, the daughter of the family stood and placed a piece of bread before the statue.

"Bless us, Binrothe, last king. Forgive us our failure to save you from the treasons of Ardin."

That shook me. What shook me more was that I recognised the mother. The creamy-complexioned maid I had silenced - that afternoon when I eavesdropped upon Robardin - had turned into a haggard goodwife.

The father looked up from his wine cup. His voice was slurred and contemptuous: "Forgive *us*? *He* should be begging *our* forgiveness for letting the mongrels who spawned Robardin get away with murder, and worse, for so long."

I had been aware that scions of the House of Ardin held a certain repute. What I had not done was put something that formed part of the backdrop to my life together with what I had witnessed. For how long had the House of Rothe naively turned a blind eye to the degeneracy of other Houses, or let itself be played false?

My former maid whispered: "Hush, Meniro. We did nothing to inform him. He could never have seen it without our aid. We let him down."

"*We* let *him* down? Woman, he died raising the nether horde that sacked Alar. They will never forgive, and nor should we, that a monarch of the Splendid City would stoop so low."

She bowed her head and said no more.

Even those who supposedly revered me would not rise to my defence when challenged. They were all unworthy of my slightest consideration. My list of innocents emptied itself, washed clean by my scorn.

Lake Hali lay placid and opaque under the light of the moon. I had no clue as to the correct ways to approach this, so I did the obvious thing – I plunged into it.

The waters of the lake were only opaque from above. Immersed within them, I found a dim luminance permitted me to see a short distance. Orienting myself from the faintly-felt pull of the moon, I headed in the opposite direction.

Some while later, I broke from the clouded waters into a clear medium. I looked about at the streamers of darkness that spiralled languidly from below, like smoke rising on a still day. Far beneath me, indistinct shapes waited. Two large hemispheres lay off to one side, and they emitted no dark spirals of what I presumed to be decay. After crossing a substantial distance to pause above them, I was staggered at their size.

"I see a pallid ghost."

I spun in the water but discerned no origin for the quiet voice.

"Who speaks?" Words formed as if I still had a body, which was fortunate; communication was not something I had needed to practise in this form.

"You are unable to see me? That is an unwelcome thing. I must be fading."

"And so?"

The voice chuckled: "Fairly stated. To you, who am I that my fading is something of import?"

"Then give me your name, that we may converse with civility. I am Binrothe."

"And I Naotalba. Rothe? A noble House, that. Wait! Bin. Bin! You died a king!"

"I did. But how long since the House of Talba graced my former city?"

"King Ebrothe struck us from the lists."

"Then I consider you to be more of a ghost than I."

"Let us not tussle over our claims to a better class of nothingness. I wait for one who can finish my work. Are you he?"

"What was your aim?"

"The end of the Houses of Char Kho Zhar, that the refugees of noble blood cease their fruitless striving against the inevitable, and finally rejoin their fallen comrades in the north."

"They are not all fallen. Some persist."

"Then I suspect they are no more than deathless remnants, gorging on atrocity to sustain the twisted wonderworks that maintain their wretched existences. The Houses were bright beyond compare. To sully their glory with time, and other such meretricious considerations, is an insult."

Whilst demented and sad, I could see how this entity's plans could be expanded to fit my own.

"Then we are in agreement. Show me what you have done, then tell me what you need."

"You see those spheres?"

"I see none such. All I see are two colossal hemispheres set into the lake bed."

"That is they. My vision is fixed in time by my slow dissolution, it seems."

"What of them?"

"They are moons."

I regarded the two immensities. It was vaguely possible.

"What will they do?"

The voice became fainter: "I am not entirely sure. But I do know that they will end the Houses. Moons about a planet have many influences. Adding this arcane pair will cause minor alterations in the way the fundamentals of life and magic interact."

Minor alterations were not my intention.

"They will also allow you to possess some measure of substantiality."

That could be intriguing.

"How?"

"Your state is something outside of death and the soul's transit. Under certain conditions, the eccentric laws that govern such exotic states permit us to become embodied. The moons will merely induce favourable conditions."

"Very well. How did you envision getting these monstrous edifices from lake to sky?"

"When I formed them, they were not at the bottom of a lake. That is my problem. What I set them for was to rise through the air into the heavens. The water prevents that."

A dim suspicion regarding the ancient reasons for the creation of Lake Hali surfaced, but it only made me hopeful. It also gave me a thought.

"Are you alone down here?"

"A fine question. I am at odds with one who claims this domain. If you could rid me of it, that would be an unexpected boon."

"Where would I find this entity?"

"It toils, with purpose unknown, amidst yonder towers."

I headed toward what I eventually perceived to be the ruins of an immense, sprawling citadel. Broken towers spewed the spirals of darkness that wove their way upward, eventually to taint the upper reaches of the lake. After some while of flitting between the skeletal remains of buildings that had become nothing but a giant, metallic tangle, I became aware of a presence. Orbiting closer, I beheld an entity of darkly luminous form engaged in strange wonderworking.

"Hail to thee, who labours so assiduously."

It spun, a quartet of arms rising in attitudes of arcane defence: "Who intrudes?"

"Binrothe, nought but an impalpable spectre in this realm. I have been in discourse with an entity over yonder who considers you to be the lord of this domain."

"He does? That is gratifying. If only I could loosen his grip upon this place, it would be a boon to the both of us."

"I may have discerned a way to effect that, or at least contribute."

The entity slid closer, faceted eyes of steely hue radiating a power that I instinctively yearned to flee from.

"Tell me more, ghost of Binrothe."

"The two hemispheres he lurks near. They are edifices designed to rise in air. This lake keeps them pent."

The regard shifted: "Rise, you say? So all that is needed is air about them?"

"Aye."

"I sense that you are a wonderworker of adequate competence. Think not of parting the waters to allow a vast column of air to descend to this depth. Think only of surrounding them with air. That should suffice."

The entity possessed an inspired insight.

"I thank thee."

"It is I who will thank thee, should you rid me of their pestilential presence."

I returned to Naotalba.

"If I were to bring air down, could the potency of your faded charms hold it about the spheres? I would need to make several trips."

I felt delight radiating from the unseen ancient.

"That I could achieve. To see my works rise would be worth the last of me."

"Then prepare your eldritch charms, Naotalba. I will return."

I shot to the surface and, once there, had an inspired thought of my own: outside of the stellar void, a lack of everything never existed. The vacation of one element merely prompted, or permitted, the invasion of another to take its place. Thus, a void about the spheres would draw in air, should it have a method of ingress. Like breathing through a hollow reed when submerged. Therefore, a charm that created a phenomenally long tube, from surface to spheres, should suffice.

That is what I spent a fair while doing. I found wonderworking surprisingly difficult in this form; it fatigued me in a way I had never experienced. Naotalba's mention of him fading, to work the charms of retention, sprang to mind: to wonderwork in this form used the same stuff that comprised the insubstantial fabric of my being. With that, I eased my effort. A thin tube would have to do. I had a certainty that I needed to be frugal, my resources being terribly finite.

Eventually, I returned to the region about the spheres.

"Naotalba, can you cause water to evacuate the area within one of your charms?"

"I can, but the pressure for that void to fill is something I cannot resist for more than a few moments."

"It will be enough. Do it."

In the water before me, a silvery sphere appeared. It distorted as I watched. Without pause, I attached my tube to it. A high-pitched shriek announced the arrival of air. The sphere ceased to distort, growing firm and perfect.

"The method is proven. Now for the tedium of scale."

Between us we expanded the sphere, placing it against the hemisphere. From there, the moon's awakening purpose bled energy that we could use to supplement our meagre resources. I know not how long we laboured to increase the blanket of air. The perceived problem of the buried half became moot, as the nascent moon shifted and rose within the layer of air, seeming only to need a bare hand-span of it about its surface.

The roar of the first sphere lifting paralysed me, and I passed through its abyssal interior, where I felt myself snag on unseen things. Or they grasped at me. Thankfully, the hooks of unknown origin did not hold. Then I was back in clouded water, as silt obscured all except the concussion of something breaching the surface high above.

"Naotalba! Will only one in the heavens be a bane to us?"

His voice was barely a whisper: "Surely not. They are set to work as a pair. It will abide nearby."

That would give them something to talk about in the city. We worked frantically, and the second moon roared upwards in a far shorter time than the first had taken to free.

"Binrothe, agent of my finale. I am near done. One last thing remains. Go to the original moon."

"That moon? Why?"

"Coiled upon its surface is one who could thwart our efforts. You must persuade the Brakung to permit my moons to remain." Toward the end of that sentence, the voice was so muted as to be almost unintelligible.

"You should have mentioned that before, good Naotalba."

Silence was my only reply.

"Binrothe."

I turned about to face the entity from the sunken citadel.

"You have removed the spheres and done for him in the process. My gratitude to you."

"I think that your thanks may be in haste. I have to go forth and negotiate with one called Brakung."

The entity nodded its head: "The Brakung will want feeding after so long. Bargain well."

I shot upward, from water to heavens, and from heavens to the void between worlds. The moon grew in my vision. As I approached, I saw that Naotalba had been understating. A vast entity was wrapped about the moon. As I approached, a bluish man-form sprang into being above the great coils and approached without visible effort, but with precipitous haste.

"Who dares?"

"Binrothe."

"Seventeenth king of the Splendid City of Gold, and victim of unavenged regicide. They call you the Ragged King now, because of the vestments you preferred. What think you of that?"

"I think that the city is only splendid in its venality. There is nothing there worth saving."

It shook its head: "Harsh judgement from one who was harshly betrayed. It is inevitable."

"Be that as it may. I come regarding another matter."

"Naotalba's moons?"

"Indeed."

"I am just a phantom splinter of that which is called Brakung. Call me Verity, for I determine the truth for it to act upon."

I knew a gaoler when I saw one; no matter how unearthly he was in appearance, or how grandly he described his task.

"Naotalba is gone. He said that the Brakung would object to his moons. Another told me that the Brakung must feed to conclude this negotiation."

"You are correct. This world has no need of three moons. Those twin blasphemies must fall."

I pondered. Far below and behind Verity, I saw a single, city-spanning eye open. Words rumbled through my mind:

I hunger. I care not for what.

It seemed that I had an ally from an unexpected quarter.

"You say that this world has no need of three moons. What of only two?"

Verity flinched. With great reluctance, his eyes met mine: "That is equitable."

"Your charge is of significant size. Would not consuming what it encircles be a better feast than one of these paltry newcomers?"

Far below, the giant eye closed and opened in an enormous wink.

Verity looked pained: "I stayed its rampage by the argument of a moon being required. Now you have given it a way to complete its task, and move on, after millennia. This will go badly for you. There are powers that watch over these things."

I looked about: "Those powers are bound by laws, and I have transgressed not a one. Brakung! Your long-delayed repast is served!"

With a roar that I expect was heard across the cosmos, the great head bit into the moon. The Brakung slid and crushed and chewed, and its tail quivered and lashed in relish. Verity spun away from me with a wail of denial. Summoned home - upon the failure of his ward - being the likely cause, I postulated.

I hung there, watching Naotalba's creations shift lazily, as if orienting themselves to balance unseen influences. Behind me, the moon lurched. The Brakung's great tail flicked as it gorged. It was upon the second of those mighty swings that the moon fractured and the tail overshot, swatting me far afield and striking Aldones a titanic glancing blow.

Time passed, while I re-orientated myself from wherever the Brakung's tail had sent me. I returned to where I thought Aldones should be, convinced I had lost more time to addled wits than to that spent traversing the sizeable distance required to effect my return.

Upon arriving at what I thought to be my point of impact - and departure - I found the void about me to be devoid of any notable features. The Brakung was gone. So was Aldones.

"You have become a blight, Binrothe."

I spun about, and found myself caught in the stern regard of the many-armed being from the depths of Lake Hali.

"One such as you has never been seen. Even now, I feel the need to assuage your vengeance still burning brightly within you, underpinned by your aching love-loss. You care not for Aldones, only that you succeed in your revenge."

"I know not the truths within your contestation. Where is Aldones?"

"It was spun from its orbit by the Brakung's careless swipe; both events having occurred long ago. Seek it beyond Arietis. You are welcome to it. The moons you freed are its salvation and damnation."

"If I am so welcome to it, why did you linger?"

"Curiousity. The bane of all thinking beings."

It closed upon me, until I could see the stars behind me reflected in the facets of its eyes.

"You have carved yourself a cursed destiny. Now embrace it."

I fled from the being's dreadful regard, speeding toward the star it had indicated. Sure enough, with Arietis far behind, equidistant between two smaller suns, I found Aldones hanging in the void. Naotalba's moons whipped about it on orbits that reminded me of a grandmother reeling a ball of cord. They tracked across its mass, and I saw that they both left filmy wakes as they did so.

Time passed as I watched. After a while, the suns either side approached close and the moons disappeared from view. They did not return until the suns started to withdraw. Finally, my interest in the vagaries of the void waned, and curiosity over the fate of those below replaced it. I descended to find Aldones carpeted in the detritus of carnage unimaginable. The awful impact and stresses of translocation had rent everything asunder, shaking down mountains and stirring oceans from their beds. Alar was submerged under an inland sea. The Nether Realms, originally nought but the peaks of mountains protruding from the waters, had tumbled, and been claimed by the sea at last. The planet had become a wasteland, with only shattered ruins to act as collective headstones for the dead.

Char Kho Zhar had only crumbled, comparatively spared the devastation I had witnessed elsewhere. There were even a few survivors. I saw a woman who momentarily reminded me of Crysanthe. Unthinking, I reached for her. She screamed at my touch, and her flesh shrivelled. I felt weight again, saw a jaundiced pallor flush my extruded tentacle. It was a thrill. I finished her and then stalked the lower city, taking anyone I could find. Screams filled a twilight reminiscent of a late summer's eve as I grew into my new self. Eventually I stopped and rearranged myself to be a biped of sorts, as the vaguely spherical form of my insubstantial state had become a physical hindrance. Then I resumed my hunt.

"The Ragged King! Flee the Ragged King!"

Their cries were to no avail, just as the walls of their hiding places proved to be insubstantial to my touch. When the lower city was quiet, I moved toward the palace. At the gates, Casiana stood, haggard of countenance and wearing the amber dress she had worn on the night they had killed me. She folded to the ground like she had on that night, but age had claimed her lissom grace.

She extended her hands in supplication as she wailed: "Golden Liege, Ragged King. Spare me."

I did not. I experimented upon her, ostensibly to further my knowledge of my new form's capabilities. Then she groaned with agonised pleasure and begged me to prolong her end! My disgust returned, but finding an end that revolted her took considerable effort. By sheer chance, as I dragged her mangled form along by the lake, I discovered the prospect of drowning was something she reacted to with genuine gurgles of terror and frantic struggles to escape. So I spent a long while letting Casiana learn how the need for air is so fundamental, you cannot deny it, even if you want to. She begged for death, told me of the places where her father would attempt to hide, whispered her secrets and dreams; but I kept her until her sanity broke.

Finally, her snowy hair spread in tendrils that shone like captured moonlight upon the dark waters. When she was dead beyond remedy, I let the corpse drift away, that corona of hair its funeral attire. The lake itself would become both her closed casket and grave.

After excavating the battered remains of my favoured vestment, and pausing to will my form into something that it would fit, I sallied forth in my colours with the Winter Crown upon my head. The last monarch of Char Kho Zhar toured his palace once again. There were a few who opposed me, and they died screaming. But within the palace I stayed my hand a little, for I sought to slaughter only one.

Robardin I found by the auras of his frantic wonderworking. As he saw my approach, he screamed and lashed out at me with whips of flame.

"Who are you that wears the robes of one long dead? Lift your mask, that I may see who dares to mock me by resurrecting the form of he whom I slew at the moment of my triumph!"

The lashes of fire passed through me. Curious, I paused and willed one to touch me. It did, and I howled at the pain. But the proof was there. As I healed the seared patch with a reflexive act of will, I knew only that which I wanted to come into contact with me could do so.

I bore down upon him, his wonderworking growing increasingly deadly, yet remaining futile. In the end, he staggered back against a ruined arch, his chest heaving and his features streaked with runnels of sweat that followed the lines graven by his exertions.

He croaked: "Who are you, damned spectre?"

I doffed my crown and bowed, low and formal. I heard his breath catch. Straightening, I set crown upon brow once more, and approached until I could see his pupils dilate in terror.

"Dear Robardin, do you not recognise me? I, who read tomes whilst perched upon your knee, and listened to your every counsel? I, who gave thee status before my court and set thee above them all? I need no mask. I am your liege."

His skin blanched in horror as his voice sank to a whisper: "No mask. No mask! Binrothe? Cursed monarch, how do you yet exist?"

I placed my hand upon his cheek, and he spasmed as the agony it caused ate into him.

"I await my Crysanthe, now that the lesser task of vengeance is accomplished."

My betrayer, the noble who brought the ruination of Char Kho Zhar, died in convulsions with my hand upon his head as if in benediction, finger and thumb clamped upon his temples. As his essence fed me, ragged wings spurted forth from my back. Since his demise had stimulated their formation, it seemed fitting that I use them to fly up and affix his corpse to one of the orbiting moons.

It amuses me that each time the moons dip themselves into Lake Hali, to replenish the atmosphere they spin about this desiccated place, Robardin visits his daughter's grave.

Eventually, the twin suns moved further away on their slow dance, or maybe Aldones traversed some circuit between them. I knew not, nor did I care. All that was important was that spirits continued to appear. Even after the translocation of my world, it still possessed its mysterious attraction. Many of the spirits seemed more confused than I remembered, but this passed in those who chose to remain.

The few survivors of my purge died out quickly, but a new host grew as I found my command of the transition from spirit to foundling undiminished.

A novel facet of this venerable custom was that many spirits visited repeatedly before deciding to remain, instead of coming with clear intent. A few came resolute, but they were far outnumbered by the ones who were almost regular visitors, before their emotional states changed and the song of the Hyades called to them no more.

This place can occasionally bring peace to the wretched, it seems.

Time has passed, and has ignored Aldones in its passing. Ages have spun by. Still the moons weave, and the stars are black through the miasma they leave in their wake. I still marvel as they rush from the sky when the twin suns attain their closest points. Two great black spheres that scream through the air, slowing so rapidly that they sink into the lake with barely a ripple. As the twin suns move away, the moons surface and ascend once again, speeding eagerly into the void with a muted roar.

Three changes have occurred due to tales about this place being disseminated by those who have merely visited, in dreams or deliria. Firstly, charlatans from many homeworlds now seek me out, believing me to be an avatar of the powers that watch. Secondly, some have discerned means to summon me to their homeworlds. Finally, a few have gained knowledge of the sigil of my House. In the first two cases, they suffer the delusion of being wonderworkers, in addition to their arrogance in seeking or calling me in the first place. As my form remains unstable and requires replenishing, survival is rarely an outcome for them. Especially when I am summoned away from the precincts of Char Kho Zhar. It makes me fractious as well as hungry. People die for causing me the slightest irritation, sometimes without even conscious thought on my part. For those with the added gall to think that they can command me, I deem it fitting they spend short period as a tormented vassal before extinction.

Holders of the sigil, whether transcribed by them or wrought upon an item in their possession, are doomed. I always reclaim that which is marked as mine, when such comes to my attention. The conditions for said are eldritch: even I do not fully understand how I come to be aware of the existence of a marked artefact.

But the very real lethality of the threat I pose seems to lure a certain type of fanatic to me. I have seen the echoes of Casiana's adoring, agonised, lust-filled eyes so many times, in so many places, and in fools of many sexes. Not one who has manifested that trait has survived my attendance upon their tawdry passion plays.

Wherever you dwell, dear Crysanthe, fear nought. We will be together again. Time is of no consequence to a love like ours. I have thought you returned so many times, only to find that, while something reminiscent of you exists in each of those women, they are not you. But every one of them has chosen to remain, and I regard it as only meet to ensure they have every chance to find their equivalent of me.

The court of Char Kho Zhar is bustling once more, and my courtiers' foundling natures allow them to dwell here without adverse effect. Many pastimes are indulged, and the wonderworkers amongst them ensure that we always have what we need. We are each splendidly broken in our own way, and that too is fitting.

I have discovered that I have a new title, spreading across the homeworlds in a manner I liken to the way that the tatters of my vestment move and twine when I stand in the shallows of Lake Hali: I do not understand the method, but I know that it is inevitable, and proper.

In time, you will all come to me. Every soul will touch upon my shores. Listen for the song of the Hyades: it will lead you here. My court is the lacuna in destiny's scheme, a limbo most glorious.

If souls are indeed finite in number, to join my court offers relief from the endless cycle of rebirth. If they are not, I host a gathering of self-determinedly inviolate souls. Either way, they form my joyous entourage, eternal and flawed, without fear of dissolution.

Until she returns, I acknowledge the repute bestowed upon me. Ennui and despair are the instruments of my will. Hollow excess and creeping alienation are the symptoms of my influence. When you stand estranged from your life, yet still aching within, my ragged cloak is the weight that oppresses your shoulders.

Until she returns, I accept the title you have accorded me: I am *Reib Al Zha* - the King in Yellow.

SAFFRON

His tattered cloak
Touched my mind
From the pages of the play

My psyche cursed
The silken touch
That stole my heart away

Life is estranged
This world has slipped,
Revealing cracks and worse

First act revealed,
Those shores entrance
Gaining hold with every verse

Silent piers whisper,
Limpid calm calls
For my repose by that lake

Lay me down
Soft pages unturned,
His masque my soul to take.

Made in the USA
Coppell, TX
17 October 2021